A Mark on History

by
Anne Schraff

Perfection Learning® Corporation
Logan, Iowa 51546-0500

Editor: Pegi Bevins
Cover Illustration: Doug Knutson
Cover Design: Deborah Lea Bell
Michael A. Aspengren

For information, contact
Perfection Learning® Corporation
1000 North Second Avenue, P.O. Box 500
Logan, Iowa 51546-0500.
Phone: 1-800-831-4190 • Fax: 1-712-644-2392

Paperback ISBN 0-7891-5320-3
Cover Craft® ISBN 0-7807-9718-3
Printed in the U.S.A.

3 4 5 6 7 8 PP 09 08 07 06 05 04

1

Lao Wai tried to eat the food before him, but he was afraid he couldn't keep it down. It was bad enough being aboard a ship that rolled and heaved during the endless Pacific storms. But the disgusting food was barely edible. Wilted cabbage and bean paste soup, and rice. Worst of all, half-spoiled fish and salted pork. And nothing to drink but foul-smelling tea made from seawater.

Chin Lim, Lao Wai's best friend, was 17, a year older than Lao Wai. Both had been born in the Kwantong province of southern China and had left Canton to set out on this long journey to America. Now Chin Lim looked as queasy as Lao Wai as he tried to eat the terrible food.

"I cannot bear the smells on this ship," Chin Lim complained softly to his friend.

So many unwashed bodies—theirs included—were crammed onto the old ship. Lao Wai was used to bathing every day and changing into fresh clothes. In his village in China, he had lived in a two-room house with his parents and younger brother and sister. They were poor, but they were always clean. But here on this filthy, crowded ship, there wasn't even a place to wash.

It was the spring of 1865, and the journey from the port of Canton, China, to San Francisco could take up to eight weeks. They had already been on the high seas for over seven weeks, and Lao Wai had seen no sign of the place they called *Dai Fou*, the big city, or San Francisco.

"Sometimes I am tempted to leap overboard into the sea just to clean my body," Lao Wai groaned.

Chin Lim chuckled. He had a merrier spirit than Lao Wai and could often laugh when Lao Wai could only frown. "The big fish who live in the sea would thank you for delivering yourself to their table," he said.

Chin Lim had been the one who had talked Lao Wai into leaving his village and setting out across the ocean. Chin Lim had even learned some English from an uncle who had come back from the goldfields of California. Chin Lim had assured Lao Wai that they would make their fortune building the Central Pacific Railroad.

In 1849, when Lao Wai was just a baby, many young men from his village had gone to the gold mountains of California to get rich. Some of them had found enough of the precious ore to return to China as wealthy men. But most were forced from their mines because they were Chinese. They were barely able to eke out livings in the leftover mines known as tailings. Most of them gave up and became laundrymen in the mining towns, washing the dirty clothes of the white miners.

Now, more than 15 years later, young men in Lao Wai's village continued to talk about getting rich in California. But not all of them planned to mine for gold. They were needed to help build the transcontinental railroad that would span the United States. But like the miners before them, each of them wanted to return to China to help his family and to marry a nice young woman.

That was the dream Lao Wai followed now. When his mother and father had wept at the dock in Canton, he had said, "There are good jobs building the railroad, and I will make plenty of money. Just think of it. Here in our village we labor for a dollar or less a week. But in California, I can make $30 a month working on the railroad!"

But Lao Wai had another dream as well. One that he didn't share with his parents or Chin Lim. Lao Wai wanted to do something important. He wanted to make his mark on history. He knew that by remaining in China, he would never get the chance to do so. The most he could accomplish would be to become a successful merchant or landowner. And neither of those would gain him a place in history. But building a transcontinental railroad in America was a great endeavor. Such a railroad would change the course of history in that country, maybe even the world. And Lao Wai wanted to be a part of it.

Suddenly the ship's horns wailed as it entered dense fog.

"*Dai Fou!*" Lao Wai heard someone shout. "*Dai Fou!*"

Lao Wai and Chin Lim hurried to the deck above, hardly able to contain their excitement. They had survived the horrible journey. Soon they would be walking the golden streets of California!

Lao Wai could not believe his good luck in arriving safely. The violent storms at sea had not crushed the old ship after all, as he'd feared. The filthy conditions and spoiled food had not killed him.

He squinted into the fog as he tried to make out the great city they were bound for. But all he could see were the faint outline of a building here and there and some mountainous slopes to the east.

As the great ship docked, the two friends scrambled back down to their sleeping compartment and gathered the few belongings they had brought. Then they rushed back up to the deck and hurried down the gangway with the others. A river of Chinese men wearing blue blouses and baggy trousers flowed from the ship. All wore long braids, or queues, down their backs, shoes with heavy wooden soles, and broad-brimmed hats. Like Lao Wai and Chin Lim, the men carried bamboo poles across their shoulders. At the ends of the poles were all their earthly possessions—matting, clothing, and bedding. They were all headed toward some sort of lodging. The broker who had gotten jobs for the two boys had arranged lodging for them as well. They were to spend the night at a boardinghouse in the part of the city known as Chinatown. Chin Lim had been given specific directions on how to get there, and he held them now in his hand.

The two boys' spirits lifted as they walked. All the gloom of the journey was in the past. The sun had broken through the fog, and the sky above them was a bright blue.

Lao Wai and Chin Lim headed down one of the main streets. Their heads spun excitedly to take in the new sights. Tall wooden buildings—some three stories high! Hundreds of people strolling down the wooden walkways that bordered the buildings. And horses and buggies flying down the dirt streets, kicking up clouds of dust.

Suddenly Lao Wai felt something smash against his arm. Looking down, he saw the runny yolk of an egg sliding down his sleeve. His head jerked as another egg smashed into the back of his neck. Lao Wai was stunned and looked around in wonder. Was this some kind of mistake? Nobody knew him here. He had no enemies. Who would pelt him with raw eggs? He looked at Chin Lim, who was wiping the remains of a tomato out of his eye.

"Chinee heathen! Cloven-hoofed Chinee heathen!" boyish voices nearby chanted. More eggs and produce came sailing in the direction of the two friends.

"Look!" Chin Lim cried. He pointed under a wagon where they could see several pairs of long, trouser-covered legs. "Let's run!"

At 16, Lao Wai was barely five feet tall and weighed only about a hundred pounds. Like the other men of his village, he wouldn't get much bigger. But as the boys emerged from behind the wagon, Lao Wai could see that they were nearly six feet tall—giants by Chinese standards. And so he began to run.

As they sprinted away, Lao Wai remembered what his grandmother had said before he had left Canton. *Beware of the red-haired white men with green eyes and hairy faces. They will hate you because you look different and wear a queue down your back. They will hate you because of the food you eat and the clothes you wear.*

Another egg hit the back of Lao Wai's leg before they were out of range. "I thought you said the people here wanted our labor," he said as they slowed their pace.

"They do," Chin Lim said, cheerful again despite what had just happened. "Those boys are just rabble. Never mind them. There are bad boys everywhere. Anyway, we are almost to Chinatown. There we can bathe and wash our clothing. We can have a good meal and talk to others. And tomorrow we will ride a wagon to *Yee Fou*, the second city." *Yee Fou* was what the Chinese called Sacramento.

"There, we will be hired to build the railroad, and soon our pockets will be stuffed with gold coins," Chin Lim added.

Lao Wai's steps quickened when he spotted the familiar Chinese writing on brilliantly colored boards over the stores. There were general stores and apothecaries, restaurants, herb shops, boardinghouses, and tailor shops. Lao Wai stared at the open storefronts. Their goods overflowed onto the sidewalks. Marvelous wares—from hams, dried ducks, and vegetables to copper pots, teakettles, fans, shawls, and chessmen. It was like their little village in China and yet so different. So much richer and more varied.

"I would like to stay right here in Chinatown!" Lao Wai cried.

"We cannot stay here," Chin Lim laughed. "There is no one here who would pay us $30 a month for building a railroad. For that we must go to *Yee Fou*."

A few minutes later, they arrived at the boardinghouse. It was a tall, narrow building in a line of other tall, narrow buildings. An ancient Chinese man answered the door and led them to the room they would share with eight other men.

"May we bathe?" Lao Wai asked the old man.

"Of course," the man smiled and nodded toward a door down the hall.

The two friends grabbed clean clothes from their bundles and headed toward the bathing room. But when they got there, they saw that there were several men ahead of them. All had been on board the ship. And all wanted to wash the arduous journey off their bodies.

As they waited, another Chinese man came in and out of the room with buckets of hot water. As each man finished, his bathwater was replaced with clean water.

Finally it was Lao Wai's turn. He exulted in the hot water as it covered his body. He felt as if he could soak there all day. But by now several more men had joined the line, and with regret he knew he must hurry. He scrubbed his body and hair harder than he had ever done. Then he rinsed off and accepted the towel the attendant held out for him.

It felt so good to be clean again—really clean. He put on his clean blue cotton blouse and trousers. He and Chin Lim gave their soiled clothes to the old Chinese man who promised to have them washed and dried by morning. Then the two friends went to the dining room where an evening meal was being laid out for the boarders.

"Ah," Lao Wai sighed as they ate the almond-flavored chicken and drank aromatic tea. "I wish Win Que were here to share this with me. She would enjoy such a meal."

Win Que was the girl Lao Wai intended to marry. She was 15 years old and, like Chin Lim, had been Lao Wai's friend since childhood. Win Que had long, silken hair and large, dark eyes. Lao Wai's plans were first to save enough money to return to China and improve his parents' lives. Then he would marry Win Que and start a life with her.

Lao Wai could have married Win Que by now. But he wanted to make sure that his wife and children never went hungry as Lao Wai's family often did. During years when floods ravaged the land, families had to exist on one basket of rice per month. They had no meat to go with the rice—no chicken or fish. Only a little salt and sometimes a vegetable or two.

Lao Wai remembered the rains falling for over a month until there was no difference between the land and the river. The rice crop drowned, and no one had money to buy food.

So Lao Wai and many others set out for America. And when he returned to his little village, he would buy chickens and pigs for his parents to raise so they would never be hungry again. Then he would he marry his childhood sweetheart.

Lao Wai slept well that night. For the first time in weeks, the lunging and creaking of the old boat didn't keep him awake. The boardinghouse and the men who slept around him were clean. The horrible conditions he had lived among so long on the boat no longer permeated his senses. And his stomach was filled with hearty food. Lao Wai slept well with the knowledge that his chance to make his mark on history was about to begin.

2

In the morning, a wagon pulled up to the boardinghouse, and a stocky Chinese man called out for Lao Wai, Chin Lim, and the others to join the half-dozen men already in the wagon. After settling their bill and picking up their clean laundry, Lao Wai and Chin Lim hurried outside. Soon they were in the wagon and bound for Sacramento.

One of the men in the wagon already worked for the Central Pacific Railroad. He was not there now because he had been asked to accompany the wagon load of new recruits to the camp.

"It is steady work for the most part," he told the others. "Sometimes if the winter is bad, they send you home until the spring. But if the winter is not bad, as in last year's winter, you can work all year. They are rushing to build a railroad to a city in a place called Utah. Another railroad called the Union Pacific is coming from the other end. It's like a race. Both sides are trying to get to Utah first."

"Is it difficult work?" Chin Lim asked.

"Oh, yes," the man, whose name was Fong Woo, assured him. "It's the hardest work I have ever done."

"Well, I can work as hard as any man who ever lived," Lao Wai boasted.

"That may be," Fong Woo replied. "But the white men who work on the railroad sometimes do not like the Chinese. The railroad bosses would not even hire us if they could get enough white men. But a white man can get four dollars a day working on the docks."

"Four dollars a day?" Chin Lim cried. Everyone shook his head at such an incredible amount of money.

"Yes, and the work is easier," the older man replied. "So the white men would rather work on the docks. And who can blame them?"

The men in the wagon nodded their heads at the wisdom of such logic.

"Just two years ago, no Chinese worked on the railroad," Fong Woo went on. "Then last year they hired 50 of us on a trial basis. They did not think we could do the hard work. 'The little yellow men are so weak,' they said. But we proved them wrong. We showed them that we were as strong as white men, maybe even stronger. Now Big Boss Charlie Crocker wants many more of us. He says that if we can build the Great Wall in China, we should be able to build the railroad."

For the next two nights, the men camped in the open, and on the third day, they arrived in Sacramento. There they were put up at another boardinghouse for the night. The following morning, they climbed back into the wagon and headed for the railroad camp.

Lao Wai was excited and nervous at the same time. What if the work proved too hard for him? he wondered. What if the white men didn't like the way he worked and fired him? How would he explain to his parents—and to Win Que?

When the wagon rolled into the railroad camp about noon, the Chinese men were met by a burly white man who snorted, "More of Crocker's pets, eh?"

"What does he say?" Lao Wai asked Chin Lim.

"He is calling us pets of Big Boss Charlie Crocker," Chin Lim translated.

"Is the white man saying we are pets like dogs?" Lao Wai asked, wondering if he should be offended.

Chin Lim laughed. "Yes, but it could be worse. At least he is not calling us rats."

Lao Wai remembered the boys who had chased them and called them names. He decided that his friend was right. Being called a pet was not so bad.

All around them, the scene was alive with workers in blue blouses and bamboo hats. Some wielded pickaxes and shovels, and others pushed dump carts. A slightly older Chinese boy named Tai Seng immediately brought Lao Wai and Chin Lim tools and showed them how to begin.

"Our job is to make a smooth roadbed," Tai Seng explained. "Then rails will be laid on top of it."

Lao Wai worked with his pickax for awhile, quickly getting into the rhythm. Occasionally he glanced up at the mountains about 20 miles away. They were the biggest mountains Lao Wai had ever seen.

"They call them the Sierra Nevada Mountains," Tai Seng explained, noticing the direction in which Lao Wai was staring. "We have to cross those mountains with rails. We have to get over them—or maybe through them."

Now Lao Wai stared, wide-eyed. "That is the only way to this place called Utah?" he asked.

The older boy shrugged. "I don't know," he said. "But it's the way Big Boss Charlie Crocker says we must go—so we go."

Lao Wai shook his head. How was it possible to build rails over such mountains? he wondered. Such work would be very dangerous indeed.

Lao Wai shook his head again and continued hacking away at the roadbed. He did not mind the hard work. At home in China he had helped with the harvest from sunup till sundown. He had developed strong muscles carrying large baskets of fruits and vegetables to market. Now he chopped vigorously at the hard earth until the shadow of a tall man fell across him.

As Lao Wai looked up, he was gripped with fear. The white man standing over him was at least a foot taller than Lao Wai, maybe more. The man was broad-shouldered with red curls on his head and hair on his face. Lao Wai remembered his grandmother's warning. He feared that this big man did not like his work. Or maybe that the man thought that he should have the job, not Lao Wai.

"You sure don't look strong enough to do such work," the big man said.

"What does he say?" Lao Wai whispered to Chin Lim.

"He says you don't look strong enough to do this work. Just say in English 'me plenty strong,' " Chin Lim advised.

"Me plenty strong," Lao Wai said with effort. The strange words seemed to catch on his tongue.

The big Irishman threw back his head and laughed. "I bet you are. I just bet you are."

He stepped closer to Lao Wai and stuck out his hand. Instinctively, Lao Wai ducked, expecting the man to hit him. But instead the man said, "I'm Terry Sullivan. I'm your crew boss."

"Take his hand, and tell him your name," Chin Lim said. "He is being friendly."

Lao Wai straightened up and hesitantly took the man's huge hand.

"Lao Wai," he said as the big man pumped his hand until it seemed it would fall off.

"You and your friend here are good workers," Sullivan said. "I can see that already."

"Thank you," said Chin Lim. He nudged Lao Wai, who echoed his words.

"You just keep working like that, and there'll be a job for you here until the railroad's finished," Sullivan said. He nodded toward a group of white men working nearby. "And if any of the men around here bother you, you just let me know. I'll take care of them."

"Thank you," Chin Lim said again.

Chuckling to himself, Sullivan headed toward another Chinese worker a few feet away.

"What did he say?" Lao Wai asked.

"He said if we work hard, we will have jobs until the railroad is finished," Chin Lim beamed. "He is one of the bosses. He said if any of the white men bother us, he will help us out. See? Not all of them are demons—even the ones with red hair!"

Lao Wai smiled and returned to his work. This is a good sign, he told himself. To be praised by one of the bosses. And to be assured of a job until the railroad was finished. What more could he ask for? He wished he could share his news with his parents. They would be very proud of him, he knew. He planned on writing them a letter as soon as he could.

As the workday wore on, Lao Wai was able to observe the rail-laying process. Railroad cars carried the iron rails to within half a mile from where the roadbed was finished. Then the rails were loaded onto horse-drawn carts. The horses pulled the carts to the roadbed, where two white men grabbed the rails and dropped them into place. It took about one minute to lay four rails.

The terrain was fairly flat so things went smoothly. But again Lao Wai found himself looking up at the mountains in the distance. He wondered how the same process would ever be achieved thousands of feet up the side of a mountain.

When the white workers' eight-hour day came to an end, Lao Wai watched them drop their tools and immediately head to the meal wagon. There they loaded food onto tin plates and began wolfing it down.

"Do the white men not bathe before they eat?" Lao Wai asked Tai Seng.

Tai Seng laughed. "Bathe? Oh, no. In fact, they sleep in their clothes for weeks at a time! But later, when we are done working, I will show you a little stream not far from here where you and your friend can bathe and wash your clothes."

The Chinese worked another four hours. At the end of the 12-hour day, Lao Wai and Chin Lim were weary and hungry. But they eagerly followed Tai Seng to the stream. Many other Chinese workers were already there.

The water was cold but invigorating. After bathing, Lao Wai and Chin Lim washed their blue blouses and pants. Then they headed back to the camp to hang them out to dry.

"I'm starving!" Chin Lim exclaimed as they walked.

"Yes, I am hungry too," Lao Wai replied. He wondered what they would have for their evening meal. The white workers' food had looked unappealing to him. He dreaded the thought of eating the stringy beef and hard biscuits with nothing but water to wash them down. But his fears turned out to be needless.

When they reached camp, Lao Wai saw a sight he had never expected to see. Vendors from San Francisco had brought food to the Chinese workers!

Lao Wai was astounded to see dried oysters and cuttlefish, dried bamboo shoots, and rice and salted cabbage. Tea boys circulated through the workers, pouring boiled tea from barrels they carried on long poles across their shoulders.

Lao Wai felt almost guilty as he ate his meal. He knew that his parents and brother and sister had never tasted such wonderful food. He doubled his resolve to send as much money home as possible. And to save all he could so that he might return to China and make their lives easier.

3 The days turned into weeks, and soon an entire month had passed. Lao Wai and Chin Lim received their first pay.

Lao Wai divided his money four ways. Part of it went to the broker in China who had arranged the job for him. Part of it went to pay his share of the workers' needs in the camp. Another portion he set aside for himself. But the largest part he sent to his parents in China.

His heart swelled with pride as he wrote his first letter home.

Dear Mother and Father,

I find this work on the railroad to my liking. It is very hard work, and every night I am very tired, but I am proud of the good job that I do. The food is good too, and I am well. Please accept the money I send. I hope it makes your lives easier. Also, please ask Win Que to be patient. I will return when I have enough money for us to be married. I have made my first friend among the white men. His name is Sullivan. He has assured me that I will have a job for as long as it takes to build the railroad. Tell

Grandmother that Sullivan is nice even though he has red hair and hair on his face.

Your faithful son,
Lao Wai

The next morning, as the men set to work, Lao Wai noticed a sense of fearful excitement in the air. The white workers were whispering among themselves. They worked as usual but kept their heads bowed as if they didn't want to be noticed. Their actions reminded Lao Wai of the people in his village in China. Sometimes a powerful government official would arrive to impose crushing taxes on the villagers. Then the people would tremble, afraid to make a wrong move for fear of punishment.

"What's going on?" Lao Wai whispered to Chin Lim. He was careful to keep his head down as he talked. "Can you understand what the white workers are saying?"

"They say there is a big boss in camp," Chin Lim whispered back. He took a quick glance around. "Look!" he said. "That must be him!"

Lao Wai peered through the wall of taller and stockier white workers to see James Harvey Strobridge. "Stro" was the 37-year-old foreman of the railroad building project. Like Sullivan, he was a huge man—well over six feet tall.

"Work harder, men," Sullivan urged quietly as he circulated among his crew. "Old Stro's got the temper of a wounded grizzly bear. And he strikes like a scorpion if he thinks a man's not doing his share."

"What did he say?" Lao Wai asked.

"Just work!" Chin Lim whispered.

Lao Wai went furiously to work with his pickax. He didn't want the wrath of Strobridge to descend upon him. All around him, he could hear the pace of the work pick up. All the men were scrambling to their tasks under Strobridge's watchful eye.

A few times Lao Wai risked a glance up. Each time he was sure Strobridge was staring right at him and the Chinese men who worked beside him. Strobridge stood with his legs spread apart and his hands on his hips. He was a commanding figure, and Lao Wai trembled under his piercing gaze.

Perhaps what he had feared on the wagon trip that first day was about to happen. Perhaps Strobridge did not like the work Lao Wai was doing. Perhaps the big boss man would fire him. Then where would he go? He couldn't possibly return to China broke and in shame. Besides, he didn't have the money for the return passage. He would be stranded in this strange land. And he would be denied his chance to leave his mark on history.

The next time Lao Wai looked up, Strobridge was talking intently to Sullivan. As he talked, he pointed his finger toward the Chinese workers.

"What is the boss man saying to Sullivan?" Lao Wai whispered to his friend.

"I don't know," Chin Lim replied. "But don't worry about it. Just keep working."

But Lao Wai couldn't shake his fears. What if Strobridge was singling him out and telling Sullivan to throw him off the job? His whole future depended on that job.

"Look!" Chin Lim said. "Here comes

Sullivan."

Lao Wai glanced up. Sullivan was headed toward them, grinning widely from beneath his beard.

"Hey!" Sullivan shouted to his crew. "Did you hear what old Stro said? He said he wished he had 1,000 more Chinese working for him. He said he never saw men do so much work in so short a time!"

As Chin Lim translated for the group, Lao Wai felt a rush of relief. Strobridge liked their work! His job was still secure! He shook his head at his own foolishness and realized that he had just learned a lesson: hard work was appreciated everywhere.

* * *

By midsummer, the terrain they worked on began to rise. In the last 13 miles before the Sierra Nevadas, the slope of the land rose 1,200 feet! The workers toiled as hard as ever. But it was getting more and more difficult to carve a roadbed out of the steep, rocky earth.

Just ahead of them was Cape Horn

rising sharply out of the ground. Lao Wai was interested—and a bit frightened—to see what the big boss would do. How would Strobridge manage the impossible task of chopping out a roadbed? Lao Wai wondered. And then what plan would he come up with for laying track across the face of the steep cliff?

"It looks like this might be the end of the road," one of the white workers said. "What are we supposed to do? Climb the mountain like ants and chop out the ledge? No man can do that. We'd have to work at a 75-degree angle. That's just not possible for man or beast!"

But Strobridge's crew of engineers said it could be done if a ledge could be carved out of the cliff. For a long time, Strobridge and his engineers conferred with the bosses of the Chinese crews. Some, like Sullivan, were white men. Others were Chinese who had been on the project since the beginning. Some of these could now speak enough English to get by.

They met in Strobridge's big tent and were in there for the better part of a morning. Finally the crew leaders emerged, looking grim. They had their orders. They came back to Lao Wai and the other Chinese workers and explained what was to be done.

"You're to weave baskets," Sullivan announced. "Strong enough to hold a man—a Chinese man. And you must hurry." He lowered his eyes then as if ashamed to look at his crew.

Chin Lim translated for the rest of the crew. Then he said, "We will make the baskets, but what are they for?"

Sullivan took a deep breath and began explaining the plan. Each basket would carry a Chinese worker. The Chinese had been chosen because of their light weight. The worker would be lowered from the top of Cape Horn down the sheer face of the cliff. When he got to the spot where the ledge was to be carved out, the worker would hammer a little hole in the rock. Then he would tamp in some blasting powder, light the fuse, and immediately signal to be pulled up. Since the fuse would already be lit, the man in the basket could not delay signaling for even a second. If he did, he would be blown to pieces, and his remains would fall hundreds of feet into the American River below.

Lao Wai and the other workers asked no more questions. Immediately they set to work gathering supplies to make the baskets.

"You people amaze me," Sullivan said with admiration. "There's not a white man on the line who would do such a thing."

Chin Lim shrugged. "We must," he said. "It is the only way."

He translated for Lao Wai, who nodded in agreement. By accepting the dangerous task, the Chinese workers would prove that they were braver than the white workers. That would ensure jobs for them and for the Chinese men yet to come. Refusing the task would mean that the Central Pacific Railroad would never meet the Union Pacific in Utah. And the dream of the railroad across America would end where they stood.

* * *

The Chinese men spent the next few days weaving strong baskets. Finally it was time to try out Strobridge's plan.

"I'll let you decide who will go first," Sullivan quietly told his crew. Obviously, he did not want to force anyone to do the dangerous task. "Talk it over amongst yourselves, and let me know."

As it turned out, every man on the crew volunteered to go first. Each felt it was his duty, and none wanted to put any of the others in danger. Finally, the men decided to draw lots.

Chin Lim gathered as many small pebbles as there were crew members. With a chisel, he scratched an *X* on one of the small rocks. Then he put them in his hat and mixed them up. One by one the men drew pebbles. They held them in their hands until everyone was finished drawing. Then, slowly, each man opened his palm and examined his pebble. Everyone began looking around, asking, "Who is it? Who has the pebble with the *X*?" All eyes fell on Lao Wai, who was just opening his hand for a look. Smiling, he held up the small rock for everyone to see. His was the one with the *X* on it!

The other men congratulated him. He

was doing a great service for the Chinese people, and each of them would have been glad to do the same.

"I go," Lao Wai told Sullivan. By now he was picking up a few words of English.

Sullivan nodded and said, "God be with you, son." Then he turned to the rest of the crew and shouted, "Ready the baskets!"

Two baskets were secured with ropes. As Lao Wai climbed into one of them, Chin Lim approached. "Are you frightened, my friend?" he asked.

"Yes, very frightened," Lao Wai quietly admitted.

"You will be fine," Chin Lim assured him. "Just do not look down. Look straight at the cliff before you. That's the only way to keep your fear from getting the best of you."

Lao Wai nodded. Neither friend said anything more. Each knew that no words could express the gravity of the situation.

Lao Wai felt a dizzying sense of fear as the basket was nudged over the side of the cliff. With a last glance at Chin Lim, he closed his eyes and felt the basket drop. A stiff wind had come up, and as the basket descended, it blew about like a kite. But Lao Wai hung on, barely breathing, until at last he felt the basket stop.

Cautiously he opened his eyes. As Chin Lim had advised, he looked straight ahead at the granite face of Cape Horn and the place where he needed to bore out a small hole.

With hands that trembled, Lao Wai gripped the small hand drill and began working at the granite. But for a long time, the rock seemed impermeable. He kept at it until finally a tiny crumble of granite came loose. Twenty minutes later, he had a hole about the size of his little finger. But he knew it had to be bigger, much bigger in order to pack in enough powder to blast away a good piece of granite.

As Lao Wai worked, he kept reminding himself not to look down. The American River was over 1,000 feet below him. He knew that if he fell from that height, his body would be shattered by the rocks or, worse yet, lost in the river. He had been comforted by his broker's promise to return his body to China if he should die in this strange land. But if his remains were lost in the river, what then? How could his loved ones make his grave and bring flowers and food to remember him?

An hour later, the hole was finally big enough to insert the blasting powder. He signaled the men above, who lowered another basket. Lao Wai reached in and took some of the fine white powder and tamped it into the hole.

Now was the moment of truth. Lao Wai said a prayer, thought about his parents and Win Que, and lit the fuse. Then he jerked hard on the rope. Instantly his basket began to rise. Seconds later, as he was climbing out of the basket, the blasting powder exploded, sending rocks and dust flying into the air.

Sullivan looked over the side of the cliff and smiled. "You made a hole the size of my head there, son!" he said, clapping Lao Wai on the back.

The crowd of men around Lao Wai, both Chinese and white, cheered. It could be done! The Central Pacific Railroad would be completed!

Lao Wai felt an incredible sense of happiness. He had accomplished a dangerous and amazing thing. He had hung over a river, defied death, and blown a hole in the side of Cape Horn. And he had been the first to do it! Surely he had paved the way for other Chinese men to come to America and work. And surely he was on his way to making his mark on history!

4

Lao Wai was lowered over the cliff to make holes many times after that first day, and each time he felt a little less frightened. He had confidence in himself and in the men above who he knew would pull him to safety in time. But Lao Wai didn't tell his parents in his letters home what he was doing. He could not tell them he was planting explosives while hanging in a basket from a granite mountain. His mother and father would only worry more about their son being in a strange country, thousands of miles from home.

Lao Wai imagined telling Win Que years from now how he had helped build the railroad. Perhaps he could bring her to America to see the great feat. Then he would take Win Que on the fine train that would race along on rails built by Lao Wai and his fellow countrymen.

"I was the first man to blow a hole in this great mountain," he would tell her as they gazed out the window of the train. He smiled to himself as he pictured Win Que's eyes widening in admiration.

But things did not go as well for others as they did for Lao Wai. One morning Lao Wai had just been pulled up the mountain after planting explosives. He heard his own blasting powder detonate and then immediately heard another blast. Lao Wai looked over the side of the mountain and was sickened to see only a few pieces of basket and a patch of blue fabric in a great cloud of smoke and debris. One of the other workers had not tugged on his rope quickly enough. Before he could be pulled away from danger, the blasting powder had done its deadly work. Lao Wai closed his eyes in sadness to witness such a sight. When the air cleared and the wind had blown everything away, all that remained was the hole in Cape Horn that the Chinese man had given his life to create.

Lao Wai knew the man who had died. It was Fong Woo, the man who had been in the wagon that had first picked up the men at the boardinghouse in San Francisco. Fong Woo had left a wife behind in China. Because Fong Woo could not read or write, Lao Wai had written his letters home for him. In the last letter, Fong Woo had lamented the loneliness of his wife. He had promised her that all her tears would vanish in their joyous reunion that would happen soon. Many were the evenings that, over cuttlefish and rice, Lao Wai and Fong Woo had shared their dreams. Now Lao Wai knew that Fong Woo's relatives would probably not even have his remains to mourn.

With deep sadness, he wrote Fong Woo's family to tell them of his death. "Fong Woo died a very brave man," he wrote. "He sacrificed his life so that this great railroad could be built." Then he enclosed the money that he and the other Chinese men had donated to the family. He knew that the money would not make their life without Fong Woo less sad. But he hoped that at least it would make it a little easier.

* * *

It was October of 1865 now, and the blasting had been going on for four months. Little by little Lao Wai's efforts and those of other Chinese were paying off. They had succeeded in cutting a ledge from Cape Horn. It was wide enough for men to stand on and continue drilling.

One morning as Lao Wai looked around him, he felt a great sense of pride. The mountainside was covered with hundreds of Chinese with picks and shovels, small wheelbarrows, and blasting powder. Lao Wai had never seen so many workers in one place toiling at such a furious pace. The Chinese had proven that they were every bit as able as the white workers. Some of the white workers had even quit and gone home when the first chilly winds began to blow. Blizzards were furious in the mountains. And the men did not want to take the chance of being trapped there for the winter, unable to work yet unable to get home. The Chinese, however, continued to work despite the colder temperatures. Lao Wai knew that they would not abandon the project until they were sent home by the white bosses.

But that day came soon enough. In November, a mild blizzard hit. Sullivan and the other crew bosses called their crews together. They told the men that they were to return to Sacramento for the winter while the trails were still passable. Then they should come back in the spring to continue work on the railroad.

Lao Wai had no reason to doubt Sullivan, but still he was concerned. "We have jobs in spring for sure?" he asked the crew boss.

Sullivan laughed and said, "Don't worry, my little friend. Your jobs are secure. Strobridge has said that he will hire back just as many of you fellows as he can!"

Lao Wai felt better at that. But still he took the news with mixed feelings. He was eager to keep going on the project now that they were making some progress. But he also welcomed some time off. He knew, though, that he would have to find a job in Sacramento. Otherwise he would end up spending all the money he had saved.

A few days later, Lao Wai climbed into a wagon with Chin Lim and several other men. As the wagon headed out of the mountains, Lao Wai's excitement rose with the temperatures. He had not seen much of Sacramento the first time and was looking forward to taking in the sights.

As soon as Lao Wai and Chin Lim settled into their boardinghouse in

Sacramento, they headed for the spot where the first railroad tracks had been laid—where the Central Pacific had begun. Both swelled with pride to think how far they had taken those tracks.

"We are part of something very big and important," Lao Wai said. "It is not the Great Wall of China, but it is a magnificent project nevertheless. Doesn't it make you proud, my friend?"

"Oh, yes," Chin Lim said, nodding his head. "It makes me very proud. But we are done with the railroad for a few months. And I am looking forward to enjoying myself. Right now I'm thinking about doubling the money I've saved."

"How will you do that?" Lao Wai asked.

"By gambling," Chin Lim answered. "There is a store across the street from our boardinghouse. Many of our friends from the camp gamble in the back room there. Want to come along?"

"I don't know," Lao Wai said. "I would like to increase my money too. But I do not want to lose any."

Chin Lim laughed. "You do not have a gambler's heart, my friend," he said.

"Probably not," Lao Wai admitted. "My gold coins are too precious to me. I could not bear losing a single one of them in a game. But I will come along just the same. I'm sure I'll enjoy being with my friends and watching you."

Lao Wai and Chin Lim walked to the store and entered the back room. It was crowded with Chinese men. Some of them lounged around reading books or newspapers. Others drank tea and gossiped or wrote letters home. But mostly they gambled. They played *mah-jong*, a Cantonese game played with tiles. And they played *fan tan*, a game played with beads or buttons. Some of the men tossed dice and played dominoes too.

Lao Wai watched Chin Lim play dice with a group of three other men. In no time at all, Chin Lim had a big pile of coins in front of him.

"What did I tell you, Lao Wai?" Chin Lim said, smiling broadly. "I have already doubled my money."

"You are very lucky, Chin Lim," Lao Wai replied. He assumed that his friend would quit then, but Chin Lim placed another bet and picked up the dice again. Lao Wai noticed that the three other men looked pleased that Chin Lim was continuing. They obviously wanted a chance to win back their money.

"Um, Chin Lim," Lao Wai began, "don't you think you should stop now?"

"Stop?" Chin Lim asked. "You yourself just said I was lucky. Why stop now? Maybe I will triple my money!"

"And maybe you will *lose* your money," Lao Wai pointed out.

"Just watch, my friend," Chin Lim replied. With that he rolled the dice. "I won again!" he shouted as he scooped up the money of the other men.

Lao Wai was amazed. It looked so easy. He was tempted to try it but decided not to. Tonight I will only watch, he told himself. I will learn how the games are played, and then another time, I will play. He spent the rest of the evening wandering around the room observing until he had a pretty good idea of how each game was played. Then he returned to the dice table to find his friend.

"Lao Wai, look!" Chin Lim said, beaming. He held up a huge handful of bills and coins. "I have more than tripled my money!"

"That's wonderful!" Lao Wai said, clapping his friend on the back.

"I'm ready to go now," Chin Lim said as he stuffed the money in his purse.

The other men immediately began urging Chin Lim to stay.

"No, no," he said, shaking his head. "My friend and I must go now. But we'll be back tomorrow night, right, Lao Wai?"

"Yes, tomorrow night," Lao Wai said, noticing the scowls on the faces of the other dice-throwers. Quickly he maneuvered Chin Lim to the door.

"Some of those men worry me," he said to Chin Lim as they headed across the street to the boardinghouse. "They look as if they could be dangerous."

"They're fine," Chin Lim assured him. "They are just disappointed—as I would be if I did not have a chance to recover the money I had lost. Who knows? Maybe tomorrow night I will lose a little—just to make them happy!" His laughter rang out through the dark night.

* * *

The next day, and for several days after, Lao Wai looked for a job in Sacramento. He was willing to do anything—unload crates from wagons, wash windows, even take care of horses. But no one seemed to want to hire a Chinese man. He could tell that some even resented his asking, as if he were trying to take jobs away from the local citizens.

Every night he went with Chin Lim to the gambling den in the store. Chin Lim continued to be lucky and urged his friend to join in the games. But Lao Wai held out. He was still not comfortable with his skills as a gambler. And he was not comfortable with losing any of his money. But by the end of the week, when he could find no job, he was starting to get worried. He was using his savings for room and board but had no way to replace it. He knew his money would run out long before spring came.

The next night when he went to the store with Chin Lim, Lao Wai decided it was time to try his hand at one of the games. He chose *fan tan* because it seemed to take the least amount of skill.

Lao Wai left Chin Lim at the dice table and nervously edged his way into the group of men surrounding the *fan tan* game. In the middle of the group was a man the others called "the dealer."

Lao Wai watched as the dealer removed a random number of beads from a box. The dealer dumped the beads onto a playing board and quickly covered them with a small brass cup. Once the players placed their bets, the dealer lifted the cup, exposing the beads. Then, with a curved bamboo stick, he began pushing the beads aside in groups of four. Lao Wai knew that the player who correctly guessed how many beads were left after the other beads had been removed would be the winner.

"I won!" shouted one of the men gathered around the playing board. Lao Wai recognized him as one of the workers from the camp.

As everyone laughed and pounded the man on the back, the dealer reached into the box for another handful of beads. Then he dumped them onto the game board and covered them with the cup. The group grew quiet again as the men began placing their bets. This time Lao Wai joined them. He bet $1.00 that the number of beads left would be two.

When all the bets were placed, the dealer lifted the cup. As before, he removed the beads in groups of four. When all groups of four had been removed, two were left! Lao Wai and another man had won! They would split their winnings.

Lao Wai let out a gasp of joy and astonishment. He had started out with one dollar and now had nearly two! And it had been so easy!

Quickly he placed another wager. This time he bet a dollar that one bead would be left after the dealer had removed the groups of four. Again he guessed right.

The other men smiled as Lao Wai collected his winnings. They congratulated him, urging him to keep going.

"No, no," Lao Wai said. "That is enough for now."

"You stop playing after only two bets?" one of the men demanded. "What kind of man are you?"

Lao Wai glanced around. The men were scowling at him in the same way the dice-throwers had scowled at Chin Lim. "Well, all right," he said. "Maybe a few more bets. But then I must go."

"Sure, sure," the other men said, smiling again. The dealer scooped up more beads, and the game began again.

Lao Wai played for an hour. At first he won more often than he lost. But by the end of the hour when he glanced into his purse, he realized that he had barely broken even. He was disappointed. He had started out so well but now had almost nothing to show for his efforts. This time when he left the game, the men hardly seemed to notice. They had won back their money, and that was all that mattered to them.

"What's wrong, my friend?"

Lao Wai looked up to see Chin Lim standing next to him. "I think it's time for me to go home," Lao Wai said. "My luck is not as good as I thought it was."

"No, no," his friend said. "Keep playing! You are sure to win it back. You must be patient. Eventually your luck will turn again."

"No. No more," Lao Wai said with finality. "I am not lucky as you are, Chin Lim."

Chin Lim shrugged. "As you wish," he said. "I'll see you back at the boardinghouse." Then, with a wad of money in his hand, he began working his way through the crowd to the *fan tan* game board.

Lao Wai stepped out of the store into the chilly night. In a way he *did* consider himself lucky, he realized as he headed across the street. He was lucky to find out that he was *unlucky* before he had lost a lot of money.

By the light of the full moon, Lao Wai could see the mountains in the distance. It looked as if snow might be swirling around the mountaintops. He thought of the railroad tracks lying up there, patiently waiting to be extended to Utah.

"We'll be back," he promised the tracks. "And we'll finish the job."

5

Lao Wai entered the boardinghouse and went to the room he shared with Chin Lim and several other men. Some of the men were asleep on their bunks, snoring softly and evenly.

Lao Wai lit a candle and sat on the edge of his bed. He took out his writing paper and began a letter to his parents.

My Dear Mother and Father,

The railroad camp has closed for the winter, so I am writing this letter from Sacramento. I am staying with Chin Lim at a boardinghouse. When winter is over, we will return to the camp to work. Sullivan, the man I told you about, has assured me that we will have jobs in the spring.

I have been looking for work but have found nothing yet. I will keep looking. In the meantime, I am enclosing a small amount of money. I am sorry it is so little, but it is all I can afford right now. I am confident that I will soon have more and will send you a larger amount later.

Your son,
Lao Wai

By the time Lao Wai was finished with the letter, he was sleepy. He blew out his candle and went to bed.

Lao Wai woke up sometime before dawn. He looked across at Chin Lim's bunk and noticed that it was empty. Can he still be gambling? he wondered. That was odd. Usually, Chin Lim was home by midnight or shortly after. Lao Wai could only assume that things were not going well for his friend. He shuddered at the thought of Chin Lim losing his hard-earned money in the gambling den.

Lao Wai tried to go back to sleep but couldn't. It worried him that Chin Lim was not back yet. He decided to look for his friend.

Lao Wai dressed quietly and headed down the stairs and out the door of the boardinghouse. By the time he reached the street, the sky was lightening with the first rays of dawn.

Lao Wai glanced across the street and saw that the front of the store was still dark. This did not surprise him since the gambling was done in the back room, which could not be seen from the street.

As he headed toward the store, he saw four rough-looking white men coming around the corner. They were walking unsteadily as if they had drunk too much whiskey.

"Hey, lookee there!" one man yelled. "We've got ourselves a Chinaman!"

Lao Wai did not understand all of what the man said, but he noticed that the others were laughing.

Lao Wai smiled nervously and spoke in hesitant English. "Hello. I am Lao Wai," he said. "We friends?"

"Friends?" a swarthy man said as if he were surprised that Lao Wai had asked. "*Of course* we're friends. Right, fellas?"

"Right, Donovan!" the others replied, laughing.

"Thank you," Lao Wai said, not knowing how else to answer them. He continued across the street.

"Hey, wait a minute, little fella!" Donovan called in a slurred voice.

Lao Wai slowed his pace but did not stop. He didn't want to ignore the men and appear rude. But he was afraid that stopping would invite trouble.

Donovan approached him and said, "I've always wondered. What's that for?" He pointed at Lao Wai's back.

"Pardon?" Lao Wai said, glancing over his shoulder at the man.

"The pigtail," Donovan said, reaching out and grabbing the queue that hung down Lao Wai's back. Instantly Lao Wai was brought to a halt. "What's it for?"

Lao Wai had heard the word "pigtail" used derisively by a few of the white men at the railroad camp. He knew it was an insulting term for his queue.

He didn't know how to explain that all Chinese men wore queues to show their loyalty to the rulers in China. If they left the country and then returned, their queues had to be intact. If not, they would not be accepted back into Chinese society. Still he struggled to keep the conversation on a friendly level.

"Queue," he said, smiling. "All China men have. I go now." He started to move away, but the man held tight to his queue.

"Oh, it's a *queue*!" Donovan said mockingly. "Excuse *me*. I thought it was a *pigtail*." With that, he gave Lao Wai's queue a hard jerk. Then he turned to his friends. "What do you say, fellas?" he asked. "What should we do with this little Chinee's *pigtail*?"

"Cut it off!" one of the other men said. He removed a knife from a sheath on his belt. Lao Wai could see the blade glimmer in the dim morning light.

Even though he had not understood what the men had said, he could guess what was next. He had heard stories of hapless Chinese men caught by white hoodlums who cut off their queues. It was one of the white men's ways of showing the Chinese that they weren't welcome in California. So Lao Wai turned sharply, catching the white man off guard and freeing his queue from the man's hand. Then he started running.

Lao Wai's mind raced. He considered running toward the gambling den but knew that if he did, he would only be causing more trouble. He had seen weapons among the Chinese men there, too, and knew that they would not hesitate to kill the white men if they felt threatened. And that, of course, would only lead to trouble for all the Chinese in California.

Then he thought about running back to the boardinghouse. But if the men knew where he lived, they might come back to get him. His only chance, he decided, was to lose them among the many buildings in the crowded city.

"Get him!" Donovan yelled, and the four of them took chase.

Even though they were drunk, they were all bigger than Lao Wai, with longer legs for swift running. So Lao Wai had to rely on trickery. He pretended to be running straight down an alley. Then he jumped aside and sprinted through a yard. It didn't take the men long to realize that they had been tricked. Soon Lao Wai could hear them gaining on him.

He zigzagged around two more buildings and ended up on a narrow, sloped street lined with businesses. He desperately surveyed the buildings. He hoped to see a Chinese business whose owners were there preparing for the day. Perhaps they would offer to help him.

But the only building that looked open was not a Chinese business. Lao Wai could tell by the tables out front that it was a restaurant. But the sign above the door was not written in Chinese.

Lao Wai glanced up the street and saw the four men just coming around the corner of a building. In another second, they would spot him. He decided to take a chance. He ran around to the side door of the restaurant and pounded on the door, shouting in English, “Help! Help!”

6 Suddenly the door swung open. Lao Wai looked up to see a young woman with rich auburn hair and startling blue eyes. Her skin was the color of the moon he had seen the night before—pale white but with a kind of glow. Lao Wai had never seen a woman with such features. She reminded him of a beautiful bird. When she reached up to move a strand of hair from her eyes, he saw that her hands were covered with flour and she held a rolling pin.

"What's wrong?" she asked when she saw Lao Wai. She glanced around then and spotted the four men rounding the building. Suddenly her blue eyes narrowed.

"Don't you four have anything better to do than chase boys?" she demanded.

"Go back to your bread making, Maggie," Donovan said. "This is no concern of yours."

Maggie put one hand on her aproned hip and tossed her auburn hair. "What's he done?" she asked.

Donovan's eyes darted back and forth between Maggie and Lao Wai. "He's a thief," he said.

"A thief," Maggie repeated. "And would you mind telling me what he stole from you?"

"Um . . . he stole . . . my watch!" the man replied.

"Yeah, that's right," one of the other men concurred. "He stole ol' Jim's watch!"

"You're a liar, Donovan," Maggie snorted. "You're all liars. Liars and drunks. Now get yourselves home before I pin your ears back good!" She brandished the rolling pin threateningly.

Lao Wai tried desperately to understand what was being said, but he couldn't. But it looked as if the girl was on his side.

"We want the Chinaman," Donovan said. "We need to teach him a lesson."

Maggie disappeared into the restaurant. But before the men could approach Lao Wai, she was back—this time with a meat cleaver. "If you ruffians aren't gone from my sight within two minutes, I'll teach *you* a lesson!"

Donovan stood glaring at Lao Wai. He was obviously debating whether Lao Wai was worth the trouble that this fiery young woman promised. The rest of the group stood by, waiting for him to make a decision.

Finally Donovan shrugged and, without saying another word, turned and walked away. The other three reluctantly followed.

Maggie looked at Lao Wai and smiled. "My name is Maggie McCluskey," she said.

"I am Lao Wai," he replied. "Thank you. Thank you."

"That's all right," the young woman replied. "Those four need to be taught a good lesson now and again. You must be one of the Chinese who's been working on the railroad."

Lao Wai couldn't understand what she was saying, so he simply said again, "I am Lao Wai."

"Do you need work?" Maggie asked.

"Work" was one of the words Lao Wai had learned at the railroad camp. "Work! Yes!" he said.

Maggie motioned for him to step inside.

Lao Wai looked around the big kitchen. A cast-iron stove was burning in one corner. Next to the stove was a double-basined sink. One side was stacked with dirty dishes. The other side was filled with soapy water.

"We need a dishwasher," Maggie explained, leading Lao Wai over to the sink. "Dishwasher," she repeated, picking up a plate and scrubbing it with a rag. "Dishwasher."

"Yes! Yes! " Lao Wai said eagerly. "Dishwasher!"

"Good!" Maggie said, putting down the dish. "Tomorrow work here!" She pointed at the floor.

"Yes, yes!" Lao Wai said. "Tomorrow—here! Thank you! Thank you!"

Maggie threw back her head and laughed gaily. "You're welcome," she said.

"Good-bye," Lao Wai said as he headed out the door.

"Good-bye," Maggie called after him. "And don't forget—tomorrow!"

Lao Wai rushed back toward the boardinghouse, hoping Chin Lim had at last gotten home. He wanted to share the good news of his job. And his rescue by the beautiful auburn-haired girl.

Lao Wai found his friend at home when he arrived. But Chin Lim was in a foul mood.

"I was robbed," Chin Lim grumbled.

Lao Wai was shocked. He had been waylaid by men who wanted to lop off his queue, and now Chin Lim had been robbed! What kind of a place was this Sacramento? "Did white demons rob you?" he asked.

"No. It happened in the gambling den," Chin Lim said. "I won at *fan tan*, but I was cheated out of my winnings."

"I don't understand," Lao Wai said. "If you won, you won. How could you be cheated out of your winnings?"

"I had been winning all night," Chin Lim explained. "The other men were jealous of me. When I said I was leaving, they coaxed me to stay. Then when I agreed, they urged me to bet all my money at once. 'You're sure to win, Chin Lim,' they told me. 'You're so lucky, Chin Lim.' "

"And you did?" Lao Wai asked, not really wanting to hear the answer.

Chin Lim sighed. "Yes," he said. "I bet all my money that there would be two beads left. But before I could check to see, the dealer announced, 'Three left.' Then he scooped the remaining beads up in his hand."

"What did you do?" Lao Wai asked.

"What could I do?" Chin Lim replied. "I started to protest, but the other men agreed with the dealer." He buried his face in his hands. "How could I have been so gullible?" he moaned. "I have lost almost everything I've won since coming to Sacramento. How will I explain this to my family?"

Lao Wai placed his hand on his friend's shoulder. "It's all right, Chin Lim," he said. "Perhaps you can get your money back. Maybe you could get a job."

Chin Lim looked up, frowning. "A job?" he asked. "Who in Sacramento will hire a Chinese man?"

Lao Wai smiled. "That is what I wanted to tell you. I got a job today!"

"Doing what?" Chin Lim asked.

"Washing dishes," Lao Wai replied. "In a restaurant."

"Washing dishes?" Chin Lim cried scornfully. "We are not dishwashers, Lao Wai. We are railroad men."

"We will be railroad men again in the spring," Lao Wai pointed out. "In the meantime, you are a gambler who just lost all his money, and I am nothing. Right now, I would rather be a dishwasher than nothing. The more money I can make here, the better off my family will be. Why don't you see if you can get a job somewhere?"

Chin Lim shook his head. "No job I could get would pay me in a month what I can make gambling in a single night. No, my only choice is to go back to the gambling den with the little bit of money I have left."

"Chin Lim, I think you should quit gambling," Lao Wai said. "Perhaps your luck has turned permanently."

"My luck never turned," Chin Lim replied. "I was cheated. I just have to be patient. Little by little, I will recover what I've lost. Now, tell me about this job of yours. How did you manage to get hired?"

Lao Wai recounted what had happened that morning.

"And this woman saved you from the white demons?" Chin Lim asked in amazement.

"Yes, her name is Maggie," Lao Wai replied. "And after she saved me, she offered me a job."

"Tell me, is this woman young or old?" Chin Lim asked.

"Young," Lao Wai said. "In fact, she's more of a girl than a woman."

A look of disapproval came to Chin Lim's face. "You must be careful, Lao Wai," he warned. "A Chinese man must have nothing to do with a white girl here in California. You will be in a lot of trouble if you start something with her. You will wish the blasting powder on the mountain had carried you away to your ancestors."

"I'm not going to start anything with her," Lao Wai said. "Maggie is pretty like a colorful bird is pretty, but I have no interest in her. How could you think such a thing? I am going to marry Win Que."

But as Lao Wai fell asleep that night, he did think of Maggie McCluskey. It was his very good fortune to come across such a person at that moment, he decided. She had been kind enough to take the side of a Chinese boy against hoodlums of her own race. If she had turned Lao Wai away, he would probably have been beaten severely by those men. And he would have suffered the shame of losing his queue. Such a girl must have a very good heart indeed.

But Lao Wai never doubted for a moment that he would return to China and marry Win Que. He had known of the inevitable marriage since both families had begun planning for it several years earlier. Lao Wai thought Win Que was lovely and sweet-natured, everything a man could want in a wife. He knew that nothing would stop him from returning to marry her. He only hoped that when he did go back to China, he would go as a wealthy man.

The next day, Lao Wai reported for work at the restaurant. All afternoon he washed dishes in the kitchen. He didn't really mind the work, and it was made pleasant by Maggie, who worked beside him preparing food and chattering away. Although he wasn't able to keep up his end of the conversation very well, he listened carefully to her. He hoped that by doing so he would learn a few more English phrases.

Sometimes Maggie would even stop and teach Lao Wai a word or two. Once she pointed to her hair and said, "Hair."

Lao Wai pointed at his own hair and said, "Hair."

"Good," Maggie replied. Then she pointed to a chair. "Chair," she said.

Lao Wai nodded and said, "Chair."

Then Lao Wai surprised her. He held up a plate and said, "Dish."

"Yes, dish!" Maggie laughed. "Very good, Lao Wai."

Toward evening, Lao Wai could hear many strange noises coming from the dining room. The big, hulking workingmen who ate their suppers there laughed and shouted at one another. Then they fought and made up. They ate huge steaks and corned beef and cabbage. And washed it all down with beer.

Maggie's father, a big fellow named Mike, stepped in whenever things got out of hand. Once he walloped a belligerent drunk over the head, and Maggie shouted from the kitchen, "Jake had that coming all night, Pa!"

Lao Wai busily and quietly washed dishes until the last customers were gone. Then Maggie came back to the kitchen and said, "You did a good job, Lao Wai."

Lao Wai smiled and nodded. He knew she was saying something nice because she was smiling. Then she handed him his pay—75 cents! Lao Wai was surprised and pleased that Maggie would pay him so much for such easy work. It was true that he had earned a dollar a day on the railroad. But that work had been so much harder—and it was dangerous. Again, Lao Wai was thankful to have met such a generous person.

All winter, Lao Wai worked at the restaurant. When he was caught up on the dishes, he often swept the dining room floor or helped Maggie clear tables.

Lao Wai enjoyed working with Maggie. She had such a warm personality. And every day she taught him a few more words and phrases in English. Lao Wai found that he actually looked forward to going to work each day.

While Lao Wai spent his time at the restaurant, Chin Lim spent his at the gambling den. Many nights he would not come home until almost dawn. Some nights he didn't come home at all. But try as he might, he was never able to recover all the money he had lost.

"You were right, Lao Wai," he said one morning at the beginning of February. Chin Lim was just coming in as Lao Wai was getting out of bed. "My luck has turned. No matter how patient I am, I cannot win."

"I am sorry for you, my friend," Lao Wai said.

Chin Lim shook his head sadly. "I have not written my family since we came to Sacramento," he said. "I am ashamed to tell them what I've done."

"It's not too late, Chin Lim," Lao Wai assured his friend. "You can still get a job and begin sending money home again. I have been able to send money to my family all winter because of my job at the restaurant."

"No," Chin Lim said, shaking his head. "I could never stand and wash dishes all day. Gambling is like a great thirst within me, Lao Wai. Whether I win or lose, I must gamble to quench the thirst. Besides, spring is almost here. Soon we will go back to the mountains. This year I have decided to save twice what I saved last year. And I will send it all home to my family."

At the reminder that soon they would be leaving Sacramento, Lao Wai experienced a sinking feeling. It must have shown on his face because Chin Lim said, "What's wrong? You look so crestfallen. Don't tell me you are developing feelings for that woman? I warned you about that, Lao Wai."

"Don't be ridiculous," Lao Wai said. "I just enjoy working at the restaurant. Maggie and her father are very kind to me. And Maggie has helped me improve my English. I can now carry on a conversation, thanks to her."

"Don't lose your heart to that woman," Chin Lim said. "Nothing good can come of it."

"I would never do such a thing," Lao Wai replied. "I'm going to marry Win Que, and that's all there is to it."

But when spring arrived and Lao Wai said good-bye to Maggie, he felt a sad longing within him.

"Good luck on the railroad," Maggie said, taking his hand in hers.

"Thank you," Lao Wai said. "You have been so kind to me."

"Well, you've been a good worker," Maggie said. "And we're going to miss you around here."

"And I will miss you," Lao Wai said. He felt the girl's soft hands surrounding his. He looked into her eyes. Those eyes that had startled him so on that first day. He still had every intention of marrying Win Que. But he knew that he had deep feelings for Maggie. Feelings that went beyond being grateful to her.

"Good-bye," Maggie said, dropping his hand.

"Good-bye," Lao Wai answered and turned to leave. But as he glanced back over his shoulder, he could see the hem of her calico dress just disappearing through the doorway. Lao Wai knew then that he was leaving part of his heart with her.

7

As the wagon lumbered out of town the next day, Lao Wai realized gloomily that he had fallen in love with Maggie. And he realized how absurd it was. In the first place, such thoughts probably never entered Maggie's mind. In fact, more than likely she would have laughed at the very idea that a little Chinese boy would love her. Their religion, their culture, the foods they enjoyed—everything was totally different. And it was even against the law in California for a white person to marry a Chinese person. So Lao Wai knew he had absolutely no future with Maggie. But still he sat in the wagon feeling sadder than he ever had. And the farther the wagon traveled from Sacramento, the sadder he became.

"Why do you look like a sick serpent?" Chin Lim asked.

"There is much hard work ahead of us," Lao Wai lied.

"That never troubled you before," Chin Lim said.

"Maybe it does now," Lao Wai snapped.

Chin Lim scrutinized his friend. "So you

do have affection for that white woman," he said. "You poor fool. I warned you not to think of her in that way. Now you will spend the whole year in misery. And to no avail. Because even if you do return to Sacramento next winter, nothing can come of this infatuation. You know that as well as I."

"I don't know what you are talking about," Lao Wai grumbled. "There is no infatuation. I told you. I'm going home to marry Win Que as soon as I have saved enough money. I do not wish to discuss it further." With that he turned his back on Chin Lim and pretended to be surveying the scenery they were passing.

The wagon was now rising into the higher elevations, into the still snowy Sierra Nevadas. It was cold again, but not as cold as Lao Wai's heart.

* * *

Lao Wai and his companions continued blasting away at the face of Cape Horn. And by May 1866, four men could walk abreast on the ledge. Now the work of drilling eleven tunnels through the mountains was underway.

Thousands of men began working day and night. They worked in three shifts of eight hours each. Some of the tunnels were 7,000 feet up the side of the mountains. And some of the mountains were covered with 30 feet of snow!

At the tunnel where Lao Wai worked, he and his coworkers had to break through over 1,600 feet of solid granite. Lao Wai hammered small holes into the granite, filling them with blasting powder and then fleeing the explosion. The granite was so tough, though, that some of the explosions barely made a mark on its surface. Lao Wai's small hand tool frequently broke on the granite. And sometimes after working for an hour, the hole was still not large enough to hold enough blasting powder for an explosion.

"Your men have to make the holes larger!" Lao Wai heard Strobridge tell his foremen. "We'll never get this tunnel built unless the holes are big enough to tamp in *a lot* of blasting powder."

The foreman urged their crews to work harder. And they all toiled with fresh determination. But still they only gained about eight inches a day.

"It's going too slow!" Strobridge raved, marching around in a fury. "Eight inches in twenty-four hours! At this rate, we'll all be old men before the tunnel is built!"

Now Lao Wai worked even harder. He thought his heart would break from the mighty effort he was putting into his labor. He felt like a mole trapped in some dark underground tunnel under tons of snow. Sometimes he could barely see six inches in front of him. But he and the other men couldn't stop now. As soon as the tunnels were finished, the roadbed would continue down the eastern slopes to the Sierra Nevada desert. And from there, on to Utah!

Strobridge finally came up with an idea to make the work go faster. He knew that they needed more powerful explosives. The blasting powder was just not doing the job. Strobridge had heard of something much stronger than powder, something called nitroglycerin. But it was banned in California because it was so unstable. No one could be sure when it would blow up.

In San Francisco, two crates of the powerful chemical had been sitting in the back lot of a warehouse when they exploded. Twelve people died. Witnesses remembered the horror of seeing the severed arm of one of the victims come flying through a third-story window. After that, nitroglycerin was outlawed in the state.

But Strobridge knew he needed it if he was to keep to his schedule. Lao Wai watched the big man pacing to and fro, wrestling with the problem. A loophole in the law had to be found that would allow him to use nitroglycerin. On the day Strobridge stopped pacing, the men knew the loophole had been found.

A few days later, Chin Lim whispered to Lao Wai, "The big explosive is coming. I see the boxes."

"Boxes of nitroglycerin?" Lao Wai asked.

"No. Boss Man Stro, he's clever," Chin Lim replied. "He ships everything separate. Boxes of glycerin, then boxes of nitrate and sulfuric acid. They're going to mix it up here to make the explosive."

What Chin Lim said was true. Soon the workers were filling their holes with the oily yellowish liquid, rocking the mountains with terrific explosions. And progress quickened.

Lao Wai was afraid of the new explosive, but he did not refuse to use it. None of the Chinese did. But many of the white workers would not go near it. Strobridge was one of the few white men it didn't frighten. He inspected the work closely as the Chinese filled the holes and lit the fuses. Then everybody would run when the explosion was ready to go off. One day Strobridge did not run fast enough. As the nitroglycerin exploded with a tremendous din, Strobridge fell backward, clutching his head.

Lao Wai saw it happen. He could not believe his eyes. Strobridge, the powerful boss man of the Central Pacific, was injured, maybe even dead. Once the smoke from the explosion cleared, many men rushed to his aid. Strobridge pulled through the incident, but he was left blind in one eye. After that he was known up and down the rails as "One-eyed Bossy Man Stro." He continued his rigorous work pace, now wearing a black patch over his eye.

The winter of 1866–67 was one of the worst in the Sierra Nevadas. But the big bosses decided to push on despite the weather. The workers often lived on reduced rations because it was hard to bring supplies in through the snow-clogged mountains. And they worked in shifts around the clock, staggering through the snow to their tents when they were done. Some slept straight through until their next shift began.

As work ended one bitterly cold day, Sullivan counted his crew members but could not find Chin Lim. Lao Wai had talked to his friend earlier during the mid-day break, and they had eaten rice together. But after that, Chin Lim had been sent with three members of another crew to work on the outside of the tunnel. When Sullivan checked with the other crew boss, he found out that the other men who were with Chin Lim were missing too.

"I must find Chin Lim," Lao Wai told Sullivan. "He may have hurt himself and now lies injured, too weak to call for help."

"I'll send some men out to look," Sullivan assured him.

But the force of the blizzard made the search nearly impossible. The men returned, stomping their feet and shaking piles of snow off their shoulders.

"We couldn't find them," one of the men said. "But the blizzard was blinding. We'll have to wait until the weather clears to do a proper search."

Lao Wai was disconsolate. He and Chin Lim had grown up together. And they had dreamed the great dream of coming to America together. But only Chin Lim had had the courage to make the dream a reality. Lao Wai would never have been able to get on that crowded little ship without Chin Lim urging him on.

Lao Wai hurried out of the tunnel to look for his friend.

"Stop!" Sullivan called.

But Lao Wai kept going. He had to find his friend before it was too late.

Outside, the blizzard raged around him like an angry polar bear. "Chin Lim!" Lao Wai shouted. But the wind was so strong that it seemed to blow his words back into his mouth.

Lao Wai stumbled through the snowdrifts, frantically searching for any sign of the men. A tool or a piece of clothing—anything that might contrast with the white snow around it.

Suddenly he felt a hand gripping his arm. "Lao Wai!" Sullivan shouted into Lao Wai's ear. "Go back into the tunnel! You'll freeze to death out here!"

"But I must find Chin Lim," Lao Wai protested. "Do you not understand? He is my best friend. He is my brother, my companion. I cannot leave him out here. I must find him. His family would be counting on me."

He tried to pull free of Sullivan, but the Irish man was too strong. Sullivan half dragged and half carried Lao Wai back into the tunnel. He set him down gently on a stool near a small fire.

"I know you want to find your friend," Sullivan said. "But we'll just have to wait for better weather. I can't take the chance of losing more members of my crew."

"Chin Lim," Lao Wai whispered, his face in his hands, "You must find your way. You cannot be lost. If you are lost, then I am lost too, for how will I ever return to China without you?"

In the days that followed, there was no sign of Chin Lim or of the three other men who had vanished with him. As the days grew into weeks, Lao Wai's loss became a gnawing pain. It was as if part of him had been cut off—the good part of him. The part that laughed and took life lightly. What would he become without it?

The rest of the winter passed with Lao Wai hardly noticing it. He spent his days in semi-darkness working in the tunnel. And he spent his nights in complete darkness, huddled in his tent under as many blankets as he could find to keep warm. The absence of Chin Lim created a void in Lao Wai. A void that nothing else could fill.

When warm weather returned in the spring, the snow began to melt. One day

Lao Wai heard some commotion as he left the tunnel. One of the workers had spotted a pickax lying in the snow. Two feet away from the pickax under the snow were four bodies. One of them was Chin Lim. Evidently, a small avalanche had occurred, burying the four workers.

Lao Wai grieved bitterly. In his mind, he had known that Chin Lim was dead. But in his heart, a spark of hope had survived. Hope that perhaps Chin Lim had tired of this hard life and had somehow made his way back to the gambling den in Sacramento. Now all hope was gone.

The broker who had arranged the boys' trip to America now arranged for the return of Chin Lim's body to China. Lao Wai knew that Chin Lim would be buried in the village they were from. And that his family would burn incense and place flowers on his grave. They would believe that Chin Lim was now happy in the spirit world and that he would be able to send down blessings upon his family.

The death of his best friend left Lao Wai with feelings of bitterness. He was angry that Chin Lim and the other three Chinese workers had been sent out to work in such dangerous conditions. Hadn't the Chinese risked enough hanging in baskets thousands of feet in the air? Hadn't they done their part by working with the explosives when the white men refused to? Should they also be expected to hammer away at a granite cliff in a deadly blizzard? For the first time, Lao Wai realized that the white bosses valued the Chinese for their labor, but that was all. What did the death of one Chinese man matter to them? They would simply replace him with another within the week.

Some of the other men were beginning to feel as Lao Wai did. One evening, Chou Lee, one of the Chinese crew bosses, gathered many of them together. He told the men something that Lao Wai never thought he would hear.

"The railroad is not fair to us," Chou Lee began. "We have hung from the sides of granite mountains and risked our lives working with explosives. Many of us have died. Yet we work 12 hours a day while the white men work only 8. And the white men get $40 a month, which includes their food. We make only $30, and we have to pay for our own food. It is not right!"

"No! It is not right!" many of the men murmured.

"Those were all Chinese men who were sent out to work in the blizzard," the crew boss pointed out. "White men could have done the same job. Am I not right?"

"Yes!" the men agreed. "You are right, Chou Lee!"

"But we are more dispensable to the railroad," Chou Lee said. "They believe that we will work no matter what the circumstances. And until now we have. But I say 'No more!' "

"No more!" the men echoed. This time all of the men joined in.

Lao Wai was thrilled at the sudden sense of solidarity among the men. All knew about the injustices done to the Chinese, but none had ever dared say anything. Even Lao Wai had been afraid. But now the brutal and dangerous work had taken his dearest friend from him. He was ready to stand up for his rights. And so were the other workers—at last!

"Tomorrow we begin our strike," Chou Lee instructed. "Some of you will remain in camp. Some of you will sit down along the roadbed. A few of you will join me and talk to Strobridge. But none of you will work!"

The men cheered Chou Lee's words. "A strike!" they agreed. "No one will work!"

A strike! It was astonishing to Lao Wai, but it consoled his bruised soul. He felt it was the only way to get justice for Chin Lim's death. The railroad bosses must be made to realize that they had hired people, not animals. Lao Wai wanted to stay with the project until the end, but not at the price of his life.

In the morning, Lao Wai was one of the men chosen to accompany Chou Lee to Strobridge's tent.

"We want more pay," Chou Lee began respectfully when the big man came outside. "Forty dollars a month."

"What?" Strobridge exclaimed. "The same as white men?"

"And we work 8 hours a day, not 12," Chou Lee added. "Eight hours good for white man, good for Chinese man too."

"Eight hours a day?" Strobridge echoed in disbelief.

"Yes, eight hours," Chou Lee replied. "Until then, we do not work. Chinese workers are on strike."

"This is an outrage! Get Crocker down here!" Strobridge shouted to one of his men. "And you Chinese! You get back to work!" he ordered.

But the Chinese did not return to work. They sat in their tents or on the roadbed all day. The white workers glared at them and called them names, but the Chinese refused to move.

The next day, Charles Crocker appeared. He weighed almost 300 pounds, and he looked to Lao Wai like a huge bull.

"I will never give in to your demands," Crocker said when he met with Chou Lee and the others. "You Chinese get back to work or get out of camp!"

Chou Lee folded his arms and said nothing. The Chinese workers with him did the same. Lao Wai's heart pounded with fear but also with pride.

Now both Strobridge and Crocker were in a rage. Neither of them had believed these docile workers were capable of striking. But before the group departed to return to their tents or to sit silently along the railroad tracks, Chou Lee said, "We are sorry, but we will not bend."

8

In the days that followed, the shipments of food eaten by the Chinese workers stopped. There was no more abalone or cuttlefish, no more rice or vegetables or fruit. Unless they wanted to eat the stringy beef or salt pork enjoyed by the white workers, they had nothing at all. Even the tea boys did not show up anymore.

"We'll starve them out!" Crocker declared.

Still the Chinese held out. They knew that if they gave in now, they would always be treated unfairly by the railroad. And every hour that they did not work, the race to Utah moved farther and farther out of Crocker's reach.

Finally, to entice them back to work, Crocker offered a compromise. The Chinese workers would still work 12 hours a day. But they would receive a pay increase to $35 dollars a month.

And so the strike ended.

Lao Wai worked into the summer of 1867, fighting avalanches and minor flooding. But even though he was making more money, his letters home became gloomier and gloomier.

Dear Father and Mother,

I am unbearably lonely. How I long to come home to China. Without the companionship of my dearest friend, Chin Lim, the days are long and without joy. I don't know if I can face another winter in the mountains.

We have received a raise in pay, so I am enclosing more money than usual for you. I know you will put it to good use.

Your son,
Lao Wai

When fall came, Lao Wai joined several hundred other Chinese workers who returned to Sacramento before the winter of 1867–68. Lao Wai had a private reason for returning to Sacramento that he shared with no one. He wanted to see Maggie McCluskey again.

Lao Wai was now 18 years old, and it had been almost two years since he had seen Maggie. Maybe she had forgotten him completely, but maybe not. He hoped that she still worked at her father's restaurant. If so, perhaps she would let him be a dishwasher again. And then in the warm, friendly kitchen, she could chatter and smile at him and make him feel less lonely.

Lao Wai arrived in Sacramento with hope in his heart. As soon as he was settled in a boardinghouse, he went to the Irish restaurant owned by Michael McCluskey. There he saw the same sign above the door, and his heart quickened at the thought of soon seeing Maggie again. He remembered every detail of her face, the lively blue eyes, the way her nose wrinkled when she laughed, her auburn curls, and the sprightly way she moved.

Lao Wai went to the same back door where he had first met Maggie. He rapped on the door, but to his surprise, a Chinese face appeared in the doorway. The young man was apparently the dishwasher.

"Um, I am looking for Maggie McCluskey," Lao Wai said.

"Maggie?" the young man said. "There. At hotel." He pointed to a large building across the street.

Lao Wai hurried across the street and walked into the lobby. There, sitting at a desk working, was Maggie, but Lao Wai hardly recognized her. Her long auburn hair was pulled back in a bun at the nape of her neck. On her nose she wore spectacles. And her face had lost its rosy glow. She looked tired, and she looked sad.

Lao Wai quietly approached the desk. "Hello, Maggie," he said.

Maggie removed her spectacles and looked up. For a moment, she didn't recognize him. Then she said, "Lao Wai! It's nice to see you again. How have you been?"

"I am fine," Lao Wai said.

"Are you still working on the railroad?" Maggie asked.

"Yes. But in winter, no. In spring, maybe," Lao Wai said. "You work here now?"

"Yes," Maggie replied. "Pa bought the hotel a few months back."

"That is good," Lao Wai said. "And how have you been, Maggie?"

"Oh, all right," Maggie said. She smiled as she answered him, but Lao Wai could hear the sadness in her voice.

Maggie put her spectacles on again. "It was nice seeing you, Lao Wai," she said, returning her attention to her work. "Good luck to you."

Lao Wai felt his heart sink. Maggie obviously wanted to get rid of him. She had changed even more than he first thought, and in small, unhappy ways. She wasn't friendly to him as she had been before. And her blue eyes were no longer lively. Worst of all, there was an ugly purple bruise on her cheekbone. She had tried to cover it with her hand while speaking to him. But Lao Wai had seen it before he said hello to her.

"Well, I'm going now," Lao Wai said. "You sure you're all right, Maggie?"

"Yes," she said. But it was a forlorn "yes," and it did not comfort Lao Wai.

As Lao Wai turned to go, a big, tall man in a grimy shirt and dark trousers approached Maggie. "Come on, Maggie," he said. "Time to go home."

The man staggered as if he was drunk.

"You go on home, Roscoe," Maggie said without looking up from her work. "I've got some work to do here."

Roscoe instantly became livid. "I said it's time to go home, woman!" he shouted. Then he tottered backward, as if the force of his words had knocked him off balance.

"You're drunk!" Maggie said scornfully.

"So what if I am?" Roscoe demanded. "I work hard, and I deserve to have a few drinks with my friends. Now, are you coming or not?"

Maggie sighed and removed her spectacles. "All right," she said, slipping a shawl over her shoulders.

Lao Wai quietly left the hotel. He pretended to be window shopping at the general store next door when Maggie and Roscoe walked by. Then he began following them in the dusky evening.

Lao Wai wondered who Roscoe was. A boyfriend? Surely Maggie would not choose such a man! Maybe he was her brother. Roscoe had red hair as Maggie did, only his was a bright orange-red.

Lao Wai noticed that as the pair walked, they seemed to be arguing. He could not hear what they were saying. But several times they stopped for a minute while one of them spoke sharply into the other's face. It made Lao Wai nervous to see such a brute of a man being cross with Maggie. He had seen the strength of such men on the railroad and knew they were capable of great destruction.

The two slowed their pace as they reached a large, white house with a picket fence. They were arguing quite loudly now, and Lao Wai, and anyone else nearby, had no trouble hearing them.

"I'm tired of your drinking, Roscoe!" Maggie shouted.

"Don't tell me what to do!" Roscoe yelled back.

"You stop your drinking or else—" Maggie began. But before she could finish, the man grabbed her by the arm. As she moved to get away, he twisted her arm sharply, causing her to cry out.

Lao Wai was shocked. He had never seen a man hurt a woman. In China, wives and daughters were treated with respect. No man would ever dream of hurting a woman.

"Or else what?" Roscoe sneered, bringing his face close to Maggie's.

Lao Wai could see that Roscoe was putting more pressure on Maggie's arm. Maggie's face twisted in pain, and she began to sink to her knees.

It was too much for Lao Wai. He ran toward them, shouting, "No! No! Leave her alone! You must not hurt her!"

Roscoe was so surprised at the interruption that he dropped Maggie's arm. Maggie slumped to the ground, rubbing her arm. Her hair had come loose and was hanging down around her face. Lao Wai could hear her soft sobs.

"Excuse me, but you must not hurt her," Lao Wai said quietly.

Roscoe raised his eyebrows and laughed. "And just who do you think you are, telling me what to do?" he asked.

Lao Wai went to Maggie and helped her to her feet. "I am a friend of Maggie's," he said.

"Go away, Lao Wai, please," Maggie urged, wiping tears from her face.

"You know this—man?" Roscoe said.

Maggie closed her eyes and sighed. "Don't get any ideas, Roscoe," she said. "Lao Wai washed dishes for us at the restaurant two years ago. That's all."

"He's awfully concerned about you for a *dishwasher*," Roscoe added. "Just what did you two *do* in that kitchen?"

"Don't be ridiculous," Maggie said. She had gained control of herself now and turned to enter the gate.

But Roscoe reached out and grabbed her again, this time by the hair. "You got eyes for any man who shows up, don't you?" Roscoe said. "Even this coolie here!"

Lao Wai watched in disbelief as Roscoe jerked hard on Maggie's beautiful hair, snapping her head back viciously. Lao Wai reached for the first thing he could find—a loose board from the picket fence. "Stop hurting her!" he yelled at Roscoe, but the big man paid no attention.

Lao Wai brought the board crashing down on Roscoe's head. Roscoe stood as if dazed for a few seconds. Then he sank to the ground in a heap.

Maggie looked at Lao Wai, her blue eyes full of alarm. "Lao Wai, what have you done?" she asked in a shaky voice. But before Lao Wai could reply, people emerged as if from nowhere. Soon a small crowd had gathered around the three.

"You killed him!" an elderly man said to Lao Wai. "You killed Roscoe Burns—Maggie's husband!"

"No," Lao Wai said. "I only meant to stop him." He looked in panic from Maggie to the crowd. Surely Maggie would tell them what had happened. How he had been defending her from Roscoe. But Maggie was now staring down at her husband's still body as if she was unaware of the others. Lao Wai started backing away.

"Get him!" another man shouted. "Get the yellow murderer!"

9

Lao Wai dropped the board and started to run. Several of the men sprinted after him. He zigzagged around several buildings and then headed down a narrow alleyway. Looking behind him, he saw that the men were not far behind.

With a sinking feeling, Lao Wai realized that the alleyway was a dead end. The men would be upon him in only a few seconds. Frantically, he scanned the alley for an escape route. He spotted the back door of a store and a drainpipe leading up the side of a two-story building. Climbing over the Sierra Nevadas had made Lao Wai very agile. Almost effortlessly, he scrambled up the drainpipe and onto the roof of the building.

"Where'd he go?" he heard a voice yell from below.

"Try the door!" another replied.

Lao Wai peeked over the edge of the roof. The men were disappearing through the doorway.

Lao Wai crouched on the roof, catching his breath. He couldn't believe what he had done—attacked a white man! And possibly even killed him! How could he have acted so rashly? He had heard of a Chinese man who had accidentally killed a white man in San Francisco. A crowd had hunted him down and hanged him.

Lao Wai recalled now what the first old man had said. The brutal man was Maggie's husband! Is that why she hadn't spoken up for him? Could it be possible that she had not wanted his help? That she actually *loved* Roscoe and was angry at Lao Wai for what he had done? The thought was beyond Lao Wai's comprehension. How could a woman love a man who was physically abusive to her? Lao Wai shook his head. Americans were such strange people.

Lao Wai looked around from his rooftop perch. There was no sign of the men who had been chasing him. It was dark now, and he thought he could probably escape into the Chinese sector. Someone would surely take him in there. But then he realized that if the white men found him, they would punish not only Lao Wai but also the people who had offered him refuge. It would not be fair to make his innocent countrymen pay for his stupidity.

No, Lao Wai could not involve others. Somehow he had to escape to where the white men could not find him. He had to get out of Sacramento. But where could he go? He could hide in the mountains, but how would he live? A few small towns were scattered here and there, but none big enough to offer much employment. Where could he go to get a job until spring? San Francisco! Surely there was plenty of work in such a fast-growing town. And he could live in Chinatown, where he could blend in with the crowds of Chinese people. And so in the darkness, Lao Wai began running west toward *Dai Fou*, the big city.

Lao Wai ran on through the night. Again, the physical demands of the hard railroad labor worked to his advantage. He was able to cover many miles, stopping only occasionally for a short rest.

As he ran, he thought about Win Que and his family in China. What would they think of him now? Hunted like a deer, in fear for his very life. He vowed that if he ever got back to his beloved homeland, he would never leave it again. He would respect and care for his parents as diligently as any son ever had. And he would marry Win Que and treat her as gently as one would handle a butterfly.

Finally at dawn, Lao Wai gave in to exhaustion. He was hungry and tired. His legs ached unmercifully. Ignoring his hunger, he walked into a stand of trees and lay down. Within seconds, he was sleeping the sleep of a dead man.

A few hours later, Lao Wai was awakened by the thundering of horses' hooves in the distance. Disoriented, he sat up and tried to remember where he was and why he was there. As the realization of what had happened the night before came to him, he felt a great sinking feeling within. He was on the run and wanted for murder!

Lao Wai staggered to his feet. His head ached, and his stomach felt as if it had been empty for a week. He had some gold coins in his change purse. But there was no source of food at hand, and he was still miles from San Francisco.

Suddenly the sound that had awakened him grew louder. He peeked out from the stand of trees and saw a stagecoach approaching.

Lao Wai did not hesitate. He knew that the stagecoach might be his salvation. It was probably coming from San Francisco, headed toward Sacramento. But after it stopped there, it would return to San Francisco. Lao Wai knew he had no choice. He would have to take his chances. He would stay in the coach in Sacramento and hope no one saw him.

Lao Wai ran into the road, waving his arms in the air.

"Whoa!" the driver called to the horses.

"You going to Sacramento, then to San Francisco?" Lao Wai asked.

"That's right," the driver replied. "We got room for one more if you want to ride."

Lao Wai paid his fare and joined the five passengers in the coach.

All of the men looked like miners except one. He was a dark-skinned, well-dressed man. He studied Lao Wai as he climbed aboard.

"You must be one of the Chinese fellows working on the railroad," the man said without hesitation.

"Yes," Lao Wai said. He nodded politely to the other men.

There were no springs in the wagon, and every bump in the road sent the passengers tumbling into one another. Lao Wai clung to his seat as tightly as possible.

"Done working for the winter?" the dark man asked.

"Yes," Lao Wai answered. He looked out the window, hoping that the man would stop talking to him. Lao Wai was afraid he would let something about his attack on Roscoe slip into their conversation.

But the man pressed on. "Going to try your luck at a job in 'Frisco?"

"Yes," Lao Wai said.

"That's where I'm from," the man said. "I own a hotel and an eating house there. Even got a reading library and a laundry."

Lao Wai nodded politely and returned to gazing out the window.

"You Chinese are good laundrymen," the man went on. "I need another person to work in my laundry. How would you like a job for the winter?"

Lao Wai looked at the dark man in amazement. He had only known him for five minutes, yet the man was already offering him a job!

"Well, what do you say?" the man asked.

"Yes, I will work for you," Lao Wai said, still amazed at his good luck.

"I'm Nathan Halstrom," the man said, offering his hand.

Lao Wai shook the man's hand and told him his name.

For the next few hours, Nathan Halstrom told Lao Wai about himself. Lao Wai learned that Halstrom was from a place called St. Croix in the Danish Virgin Islands. He also learned that Halstrom had been in San Francisco for several years and was very successful there. Halstrom told him other things about himself, but Lao Wai did not understand it all. Throughout the conversation, he simply nodded politely and offered an occasional comment.

"Sacramento ahead!" the stagecoach driver suddenly called down to the passengers.

Lao Wai's heart beat faster. Talking with Halstrom had distracted him for a while. Now he had to face the fact that they were entering Sacramento—where he was probably wanted for murder. What if the stagecoach was searched? What would he do?

Suddenly he remembered something. The stagecoach stopped across the street from the McCluskeys' restaurant—in front of the hotel Maggie had been working at! If she was around, she would surely see him. Perhaps he should get off the coach now, before they entered the city. He could try to make it to San Francisco on foot. But then Halstrom would be suspicious. And Lao Wai would probably lose the job the dark man had offered him. He decided to lie low in the stagecoach and hope to pass through the city unnoticed.

A few minutes later, the driver stopped the coach in front of the hotel. Almost immediately, two men peered in. One of them spotted Lao Wai and frowned. "Who's the Chinaman?" he asked.

"My laundryman," Nathan Halstrom

said, leaning forward so that they could see his face in the light.

The men looked surprised. "Begging your pardon, Mr. Halstrom, sir," one said. "We didn't know it was you."

"Quite all right," Halstrom replied, leaning back in his seat.

Lao Wai was impressed. The dark man was well known in Sacramento as well as in San Francisco.

Lao Wai peered out the window of the coach, while keeping his face as hidden as possible. Everything looked normal. Men lounged around the front of hotel. Wagons rumbled by. Some men rode up on horses and mules. Two men from the stagecoach got off and another got on.

Even so, Lao Wai wished the coach would get moving. He kept sneaking glances into the lobby of the hotel every time someone passed through the door. He was afraid to see Maggie. Yet at the same time, he found himself wishing he could catch a glimpse of her again. He knew that once he left Sacramento, he would probably never be able to return. And he thought it would be nice to see her flashing eyes and beautiful hair one last time.

Suddenly the door opened, and two figures appeared. It was Maggie on the arm of Roscoe Burns. Roscoe's head was bandaged, and Maggie seemed to be sympathizing with him. She kept reaching up, tenderly touching his bandage. Once she even kissed her fingers and then touched them to Roscoe's head. Roscoe draped his arm around her waist, and the two disappeared down the street.

Lao Wai sighed. So she *does* love Roscoe. And perhaps in his own way, Roscoe loves her. He hoped the two would be very happy. He doubted it. But he hoped they would.

At least I'm not wanted for murder, Lao Wai thought as the stage left town. They may have been looking for him for injuring Roscoe. But he figured that if they hadn't found him in a few days, they would give up the search. There were plenty of dangerous outlaws in the city to keep the lawmen busy. He doubted that they would look much farther than Sacramento for him. And even if they did, it would be nearly impossible to find him where he was going.

As soon as Lao Wai arrived in San Francisco, he went to Chinatown to find a boardinghouse. Then he set out to explore the area.

Lao Wai was thrilled to be among his own people again. He almost wept when he saw Chinese people milling around in their native costumes, men with long queues down their backs, bustling around. Lao Wai did not know a single person, but they all seemed like family to him. He watched the vegetable peddlers carrying deep baskets of greens, fruits, and melons on poles balanced on their shoulders. He listened to customers haggling with shopkeepers. At one point, he stopped for a moment and closed his eyes. He allowed the wonderful babble of his countrymen's voices to fall on him like a cleansing rain. The chatting, the laughter, even the arguing were a symphony to his ears.

Lao Wai wandered the brightly lit streets of Chinatown all evening. Finally, he found himself standing in front of a clothing store. As he gazed through the windows at the various wares, he noticed several men come and go through a door at the back of the store. He realized that the store had a gambling den in back, just like the one in Sacramento.

Lao Wai made his way to the door and followed another man in. The sights and sounds of the place reminded him of Chin Lim. He remembered cheering his friend on when he won and then later scolding him for gambling when his luck changed. Lao Wai shook his head sadly and felt the loss of Chin Lim all over again.

"What's wrong, little brother?" asked a man who was standing nearby.

"It is a sad life for me here," Lao Wai said.

"Sad? In what way?" asked the man.

"I am lonely for my home in China," Lao Wai sighed. "Lonely for my family and for the girl I will marry. I think of home and the happy times there, and my heart aches. We were often hungry, and sometimes the floods swept our home away, but there was never such pain in my heart there."

The other man, who introduced himself as Wong Ling, nodded in understanding. "I have been here for 15 years," he said. "The first year I was here, I tried to work a gold claim in the mountains, but the white men chased me away. They said I must pay a big tax to look for gold, yet they paid no tax . . ."

"Why do the Americans hate us so?" Lao Wai asked. "Why do they make laws against us? We cannot become American citizens. We cannot even bring our women here to marry."

"They don't really hate us," Wong Ling said. "They just don't understand us. And some are afraid. We work hard, and they feel inferior. But we must not waste our time and strength asking such questions. We must work without ceasing and become successful."

"Well, I haven't succeeded yet," Lao Wai said.

"But you will," Wong Ling assured him. "It has taken me 15 years, but I am now the owner of a fine restaurant here in Chinatown. Just keep working. Success will find its way to you."

"Thank you for the words of encouragement," Lao Wai said as he told his newfound friend good-bye.

But he didn't feel encouraged as he went to bed that night. He thought about what awaited him in the morning—piles of dirty laundry. He went to sleep wondering how doing white men's laundry could possibly make him successful.

In the morning, Lao Wai reported to Halstrom's hotel for work. As expected, piles of dirty laundry waited for him. An older Chinese man showed Lao Wai how the work was done. "And you must be very careful," the older man warned. "If the garments are damaged in any way, the white men will not pay.

"Sometimes they will accuse of you damaging or stealing their clothing even though you did nothing wrong," the man continued. "You must never argue with them. Be polite and go about your duties."

The work began at seven in the morning and continued until seven at night. Lao Wai washed the clothing while the older man did the ironing.

The clothing mostly belonged to white miners who came from the mountains to San Francisco to celebrate a claim. Or it belonged to gentlemen like Nathan Halstrom. The miners were often drunk when they dropped off and picked up their clothing. As the older man had warned, they cursed Lao Wai and accused him of stealing some of the garments or trying to cheat them. Lao Wai endured the abuse quietly as he had been told to do.

A few times Lao Wai was excused from his duties to run errands for Nathan Halstrom. He sent Lao Wai to inspect food shipments at the docks to make sure the shippers were sending fresh fruits and vegetables to Halstrom's restaurant. Halstrom was pleased with his work both as a laundryman and a messenger. And he often told Lao Wai so.

"My boss is a most amazing man," Lao Wai told Wong Ling one Friday evening after the laundry had closed. "He never yells at me. He compliments me on my work and asks me to do more important tasks for him."

"What is the nationality of this man?" Wong Ling asked.

"He is from the Virgin Islands. He told me that his mother was an African but not his father," Lao Wai replied. "He is a grand man. He dresses very nicely, and he is as clean as the Chinese. He rides in a nice carriage and never curses or spits tobacco juice. He does not drink whiskey at all but only a little wine."

Wong Ling smiled and said, "He sounds like a good man. I would advise you to continue working for him."

"But I'm going back to the railroad in the spring," Lao Wai said. "And I heard they are going to pay bonuses to the men who will work longer hours. The big bosses want to be sure to make it to Utah in time."

Wong Ling shrugged. "The bonus pay would be nice. But building the railroad is dangerous work. I have heard what you workers do. At least if you work for Halstrom, your family will see you alive again."

There was truth in what Wong Ling had said, Lao Wai admitted to himself. If he stayed in San Francisco, it would take him a little longer to make enough money to go back to China. But at least he would be alive.

Which was more desirable? he asked himself. To die a young man who had accomplished something monumental? Or to die an old man whose accomplishments were insignificant?

10

Within a few weeks, Lao Wai was going to the docks with Halstrom to inspect shipments of silks and hotel furniture. And his confidence was rising every day. Lao Wai no longer toiled in the laundry. Every day he rubbed elbows with important people in San Francisco. He gave orders to others and made weighty decisions. His contact with so many English-speaking people improved his language skills dramatically. Lao Wai could now easily hold a conversation with a white person. He shared his good fortune in a letter to his parents.

Dear Father and Mother,

I have a very fine position with Mr. Nathan Halstrom for the winter. He is a very successful businessman and a gentleman. I have been given much responsibility. As soon as possible, I will return to China to marry Win Que.

Your son,
Lao Wai

Toward the end of the winter, Nathan Halstrom called Lao Wai into his office in the hotel. Lao Wai was a little worried. He had never been called into Halstrom's office before. He wondered if he had done something wrong—made a bad decision or given the wrong order, perhaps.

But Halstrom smiled at him when he entered the room. He graciously ushered Lao Wai to a chair.

"Lao Wai," Halstrom began. "I am very pleased with your work. You have proven yourself to be a competent and intelligent worker."

"Thank you," Lao Wai replied.

"I know your plans are to return to the mountains in a few weeks," Halstrom continued. "But I was wondering if you'd consider staying on here with me permanently."

Lao Wai raised his eyebrows in surprise. "Do you mean forever?" he asked.

Halstrom laughed. "If you'd like, yes," he said. "But I don't expect you'd want to. What I meant was until you had made enough money to go back to China. So instead of returning to your railroad job, you would stay in San Francisco and work for me. I need a right-hand man, and I think you're just the person. Needless to say, there would be a sizable raise in it for you. I'll pay you $40 a month."

Lao Wai was shocked. Forty dollars a month! That was more than he would ever make on the railroad—even with bonuses. He would be a fool to turn down such a generous amount. And there would be no danger involved.

"Well, what do you say, Lao Wai?" Halstrom asked.

Lao Wai opened his mouth to say "yes." But the word stuck on his tongue. It was as if he were just learning English again—he could not form the word. He reminded himself that his plans had always been to see the railroad project through to the end. After all, one of his dreams was to accomplish something significant in his life. And helping to build the Central Pacific was probably the only chance he would get to realize that dream. But it could also kill him, he knew. Suddenly the question he had asked himself earlier came back to him: *Which was more desirable? To die a young man who had accomplished something monumental?*

Or to die an old man whose accomplishments were insignificant? And suddenly Lao Wai knew the answer.

"I appreciate your offer, Mr. Halstrom," he said, standing up to leave. "But I came here to build a railroad, and that is what I must do."

"Well, I'm sorry to hear you say that, Lao Wai," Halstrom replied. "But I understand. And I admire you—and all of your countrymen—for what you are doing here. Our country will be a greater nation because of your efforts." He extended his hand to Lao Wai and shook it warmly. "Good luck to you, my boy," he said.

Lao Wai finished out the winter with Nathan Halstrom. Then, the first week of March, he went to Sacramento to catch a wagon to the railroad camp. He knew he had nothing to fear from the lawmen in Sacramento. And while in the city, he made no attempt to see Maggie. She was part of his past now. Win Que, on the other hand, was part of his future. If he survived the year with the railroad, he would return to China to marry her.

The loneliness of losing Chin Lim and being away from China was still with him. But now, absorbed in the hard work of building the railroad, he could endure it until the time came for him to go home.

All 11 summit tunnels were finished now, and the crews were heading down the eastern side of the mountains into Nevada. Even though it was spring, the slopes were still covered with deep snow. The snow had to be cleared before any track could be laid. So 400 horses and carts were brought in to haul the snow away. Lao Wai and the others shoveled snow into the carts all day. The first few days nearly killed Lao Wai. He had gotten out of condition while working for Halstrom. After spending 12 hours moving snow, he could barely stand or hold a shovel. But he was grateful for one thing. He had no time—or energy—to be lonely. When he wasn't working, he was sleeping. And when he wasn't sleeping, he was working. There was never any free time to dwell on his loneliness.

* * *

That year, nearly 10,000 Chinese, 1,000 white men, and scores of American Indians toiled for the Central Pacific. When summer came, they labored in the heat of the Nevada desert. Temperatures soared to 120 degrees. Lao Wai saw some of his companions pass out from the heat, be revived with tea, and then resume working. Water wagons shuttled back and forth, bringing a constant supply of water to the men and horses. Sometimes the wagons came from 40 miles away.

"Hot-season pay for all the men," Crocker announced, urging the men to keep working no matter how hot it became. Lao Wai had never felt such heat. It was as if the world were on fire and he was trapped in the center of it. Still, Crocker shouted, "Speed up, speed up!" And Lao Wai worked harder, wanting to earn as much golden coin as possible.

When the track had been laid 20 miles beyond Reno, a train arrived. It had traveled across the Sierra Nevadas using the ledge on Cape Horn. Lao Wai marveled as the train rolled in. He remembered how he had hung from baskets to form the ledge over which these passengers had just moved! He listened to the passengers as they got off the train.

"It was incredible," a man said. "I looked from the windows and was amazed that a railroad could travel through such mountains. I kept asking myself, how could they lay down tracks?"

Another man said, "I have traveled the world, and this is the greatest engineering feat I have ever seen."

In the winter of 1868–69, as the Central Pacific and Union Pacific raced toward each other, the Central Pacific crew stopped to build a hotel in Elko, Nevada. White workers went to the saloons that sprung up in town until Jim Strobridge, who was against drinking, put a stop to their pleasures. The two railroads were to meet at Promontory Point, Utah, on May 10, 1869. And Strobridge wanted to make sure that every man was able to devote 100 percent of his strength to the task.

The following spring, Crocker began pitting his Chinese "pets" against the Irish "terriers" of the Union Pacific. He offered bonuses for miles of track laid. The Irish workers laid six miles of track in one day. Crocker offered his Chinese crews a bonus if they could lay seven. They worked 16 hours a day, but they did it.

Then the big bosses of the two railroads began making bets with each other. In one day, a crew with the Union Pacific laid seven and a half miles of track, setting a new record. Charles Crocker bet that his workers could lay ten. If they did it, Crocker stood to win $10,000. But the condition was that the finished track had to be sound, strong enough to support a train

Crocker and Strobridge personally chose the men to set the record. Lao Wai was thrilled to be among them. If they were successful, each man would get four days' wages in gold on top of his regular pay.

Just before dawn on April 28, equipment was feverishly put into place for the frantic pace of the day. Some men would unload the rails. Others would place ties, and still others would push handcars.

Of the 850 men involved, 400 were Chinese. Lao Wai was one of the tampers. He would be part of the long lines of Chinese standing in the middle and on both sides of the ties. They would smash the ballast, making two gravel-crunching tamps before hurrying on. The gravel ballast then had to be packed snugly around the railroad ties to keep them in place.

At dawn the whistle sounded, shattering the stillness. In the chilly dampness, Lao Wai and his companions sprung into motion. The air sounded with noise as rails were thrown down and spiked. Each handcar carried 16 rails and a keg each of bolts and spikes. A man atop each car threw down the rails, while other men passed out bolts and spikes.

Crocker watched it all approvingly. "No man stops!" he bellowed. The whole group moved like a single man, everyone knowing his job and doing it with precision.

Two hundred and forty rails were laid in one minute and twenty seconds! The workers moved to a rhythm, spiking and tamping, spiking and tamping without a pause.

During the lunch break, Lao Wai and his coworkers ate heartily and drank a lot of boiled tea. When the whistle blasted everyone back to work, the incredible march continued.

At 1:30 in the afternoon, six miles of track had been laid. Observers from the Union Pacific watched with growing trepidation, fearing that the ten-mile goal would be reached.

When dusk came, the whistle blew and all work stopped. The men had laid 10 miles and 56 feet of track! This was an amazing feat, considering that only 50 miles of track were laid in the first 2 years of the project! Immediately Crocker ordered a heavy locomotive to roar down the newly laid tracks to prove they were sound. They passed the test easily.

Crocker had won his bet. All the exhausted but proud railroad men were given their four days' bonus pay in gold coin. Every man celebrated, congratulating one another without regard to race. During these gleeful moments, Lao Wai felt that he had truly made another mark on history.

***

At 11:00 in the morning on May 10, 1869, the Central Pacific and the Union Pacific met at Promontory Point, Utah. At last the United States was joined by rails from the Atlantic to the Pacific.

Two locomotives sat face to face on the tracks—the *Jupiter* of the Central Pacific and *No. 119* of the Union Pacific. The day was bright and cold, and Lao Wai was surprised to see so many different kinds of people gathered for the Gold Spike ceremony. Indians in native dress and Mexican men in silver-edged costumes stood side by side with soldiers, a marching band, and white men in fine suits. Along with these were a marching band and many reporters with cameras.

Eight Chinese men were chosen for the honor of laying the final rail in place.

Lao Wai was one of them. He dressed in his clean blue blouse and trousers and lined up in front of the crowd. Surely now it will be clear to others how much the Chinese workers have contributed to this great project, he thought.

But as Lao Wai looked out at the sea of faces, he wondered what they were really thinking. Did they know of the many Chinese workers who had been blown up while planting explosives or frozen to death during the grueling winters? Did they feel they owed a debt to the Chinese for sacrificing so much to build the railroad? Would they now relent on their cruel laws and allow his people to become American citizens with all the rights and privileges of Americans? Or didn't they think about all of the work the Chinese did? Or if they did, did they even care?

Suddenly, over the soft murmur of the waiting crowd, Lao Wai heard somebody call out, "Shoot!"

One of the Chinese men beside Lao Wai cried out in fear, "Run!"

Lao Wai scattered with the others. All

were shocked and bewildered. Why would the white men want to shoot the Chinese who were about to lay the last rail?

Suddenly Lao Wai heard laughter from the crowd.

"Pictures!" Jim Strobridge said. "They only want to shoot your pictures!"

Lao Wai and the others scrambled back to their places. Everyone in the crowd started laughing. Lao Wai felt his cheeks burning with embarrassment, but he did his best to carry on.

The eight men carried a length of beautiful polished laurel wood to Jim Strobridge, and he set the tie in place. Lao Wai and the others then tapped in spikes. And the transcontinental railroad was finished.

The day was filled with celebration. The palace car of one of the trains overflowed with food and fine wines. A ball was held in a huge tent for the dignitaries of the two railroads. The workers—Indians, white men, and Chinese—toasted one another as brothers. And through it all, the band played on.

* * *

With the completion of the railroad, Lao Wai finally felt that he had made his place in history. He left Promontory Point, Utah, and made his way back to San Francisco. Many of the other Chinese railroaders continued working with Strobridge on the other western railroads, but Lao Wai had had his fill of this work. He had saved enough money to return home with honor. He was ready to go back to China.

In San Francisco, he said good-bye to Nathan Halstrom and to his friend Wong Ling. Then he boarded the first boat that would take him to China.

When Lao Wai arrived at his village, his family and Win Que were waiting for him on the dock. They were all proud of what he had accomplished in America. And Lao Wai felt a deep sense of satisfaction as he showed them the money he had saved.

That summer, Lao Wai was married to Win Que. She wore a red silk dress embroidered with a phoenix, a mythological bird. And they had a great feast in the village where they had been born.

Five years later, Lao Wai, Win Que, and their small son visited San Francisco. The three rode the great *Atlantic Express* from California to Nebraska. Finally Lao Wai could show his wife and son the incredible engineering project he had been a part of. As the locomotive climbed the Cape Horn grade and moved through the tunnels, he described the work he had done with pride.

Over the years, Lao Wai often visited the grave of Chin Lim. With tears in his eyes, he would describe his part in the completion of the transcontinental railroad to his friend. "I made my mark on history, Chin Lim," he would say. "And I will die an old man who, as a young man, accomplished something monumental. Truly my luck has changed for good."

PASSAGES to History Novels by Anne Schraff

And We Will Be No More
The Bloody Wake of the *Infamy*
Darkness
Dear Mr. Kilmer
Dream Mountain
Freedom Knows No Color
The Greatest Heroes
Hear That Whistle Blow
Someday the Sun Will Shine Again
Strawberry Autumn
Wait Until Spring
Winter at Wolf Crossing
The Witches of Northboro